KNOW SEEDS

A novella by

Daniel Julaton

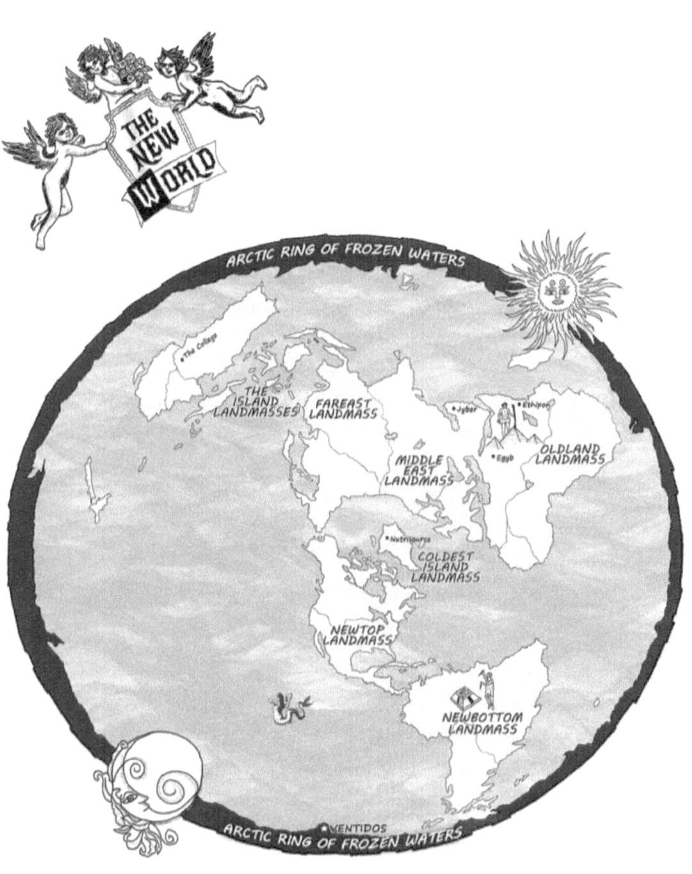

THE NEW WORLD
ARCTIC RING OF FROZEN WATERS
The College
THE ISLAND LANDMASSES
FAREAST LANDMASS
Jyber
Ethipon
OLDLAND LANDMASS
MIDDLE EAST LANDMASS
Eqyb
Nutrisource
COLDEST ISLAND LANDMASS
NEWTOP LANDMASS
NEWBOTTOM LANDMASS
VENTIDOS
ARCTIC RING OF FROZEN WATERS

Formatting: Andrea Reider
Cover art: Phil Poole
Map: Zainab Sajjad

ISBN 978-1-7353246-0-9 (hardcover)
ISBN 978-1-7353246-4-7 (paperback)
ISBN 978-1-7353246-7-8 (ebook)

Library of Congress Control Number: 2020916719.

Published by Daniel Julaton

www.knowseeds.com

For All of Us.

That at the name of Jesus Christ every knee should bow and all of our names be found written in the book of life.

"For we wrestle not against flesh and blood, but against principalities, against powers, against the rulers of darkness of this world, against spiritual wickedness in high places."

Ephesians 6:12

Preface

Based off of the conversation I had with my cousin, Jon Martinez, on 4/24/2020, about being "blindfolded." He told me not to write a book during our discussion. I reluctantly agreed. We had talked over the phone for a total of 3 hours and 13 minutes.

On 5/03/2020 at 5:33pm Hawaii Time, and after long consideration, I decided against what we had discussed. He was not the first person to advise against me writing the contents of this book. I had already handwritten the blueprint and started the book that would become *Know Seeds*, the year before.

I already knew what I needed to say, and I knew how I was going to say it.

Introduction

I have never been a fan of scary movies. It wasn't that they scared me to death, but the way I felt while watching them always made me uncomfortable. It seemed to me like the directors of scary movies always knew how to reach inside of me, to where the gut feeling was located that could sense something was wrong or that someone was watching from behind. Then they hit me with an extra dose of discomfort that would last a couple of days. Although my only real fear in life was germs, scary movies have always had a way of transferring extra amounts of unnecessary discomfort into my life. They made me extra paranoid. I avoided them like I would the plague or anything that resembled the plague.

These days are even scarier to me. It's like the scariest movie jumped from the screen. The year is 2020, and my worst nightmare has come alive. Scarier than any thriller I have seen to date. The entire world is in a state of suspense, waiting to return to normal and hopefully recover from a pandemic that supposedly came out of nowhere. The pandemic destroyed the world economy. Many people have died who did not have to die. Though not nearly as many deaths occurred, as in pandemics of the past, still the whole world is locked down to stop the spread. This has never happened before. They say it's for our safety. There is no vaccine or medicine—nowadays not many people trust those anyway. We can feel that something is wrong, but we don't know what. We only know what we are told. Not many people will ever know the pandemic was part of an ancient plan devised thousands of years ago. Not many people care to know anyway.

The bad news is we are all gonna suffer. The Great Temple is being rebuilt as we speak. The good news is The Savior knows the outcome.

Chapter 1

I sat for over an hour staring at the computer monitor thinking about what to write. For the last few months, I'd been working hard on my thesis so I could finally graduate college after a five-year stint. Booze, women, and parties have never paid the bills, and if I wanted to survive in this day, I needed to get serious about making money. Quick. The only way that I knew how to make more money had been preached to me by my parents and taught in every school I had ever attended since grade school like it was the only option available—get a degree.

I thought it was funny because my parents did not have a degree, and yet they were able to successfully provide a decent living for both my older brother and me. Where had they learned that a degree was worth anything? All I knew was that other Landmasses provided a free education for their aspiring citizens, while I had so much debt riding on my shoulders from all of my student loans that it worried me how I would ever be able to repay it with a degree in World History from The College. All this debt, and the only thing that I had learned throughout my career as a professional student was that I needed to read a lot of books. That was a good thing because I actually enjoyed reading. But why all this debt just to read books?

In hindsight, I should have just opened a small bookshop instead. But it was too late for that. I owed the Establishment of Newtop Landmass thousands of dollars in student loans, and graduation was right around the corner. I eventually figured that since I had done all this assigned reading, I might as well write down all that I had learned and start making some real money. I planned to write a book. But not just any book. I was going to write a book that would measure up to the Old Book.

Most authors probably felt as I did in that moment, I thought. Except they were too afraid to write what I was about to write.

~

Henry Gomez's History Thesis:

Since the beginning of time, as we call it, human beings have always tried to understand our existence.

Before the Great Drowning, as it is called in every sacred and non-sacred text across our flat planet, there was the Agreement. No matter who you were or where you were from, we all agreed that our existence was connected to the One High Universal Being. We called that One High Universal Being, "HUB." HUB created everything perfectly and even imperfectly, for a purpose, but it was agreed that HUB created all things. Along with every creation, HUB created the Innumerable Lights, also known as angels. Of course, HUB knew their number, but to any other creature, there were too many Innumerable Lights in the sky to count. The Innumerable Lights served HUB, and they also served HUB's creations, no matter how big or small.

The Innumerable Lights were very knowledgeable. One could say they knew too much, but HUB knew all things about everything. HUB knew how many blades of grass existed at any given moment, from the beginning of time to present day and beyond, and furthermore, he knew each and every single blade of grass by name. HUB knew beginning to end. More importantly, HUB knew the name of The Savior before he was ever mentioned.

With that said, it was no surprise to HUB that among the Innumerable Lights, there were twenty-two that would create their own agreement. The Ventidos, as they were referred to in only a few of the old texts, were the reason the world was, and still is, corrupted. They were responsible for the destruction of the First Couple and the shrouding of the First World, which no one can access anymore accept through belief in The Savior. Nothing is sacred amongst the Ventidos, and their time for atonement is nearing. They were the leaders of the group—the group of two hundred fallen lights known as the Sinpaz.

Nowadays, the First World is lost to most of the population. Nobody believes in it like they used to. Even worse, many have never heard of it because it is no longer mentioned in any of the texts. Mention the First World and all one hears is, "What's the First world?" or "Is that the place where dragons live?" like it was some fairytale out of Old Hendrix's Bedtime Stories.

It's crazy that we can all agree upon the Great Drowning, but few can agree upon HUB and the First World. The Savior is mentioned a lot in the Old Book. He is the reason the Old Book exists. But nobody knows much about the Ventidos, which were only mentioned in one sentence out of the entire Old Book. The Agreement recognized long ago is now scattered into many different theories and religions so much that nowadays we all agree upon what is known as the Many Agreements.

The Many Agreements are governed by the Establishment, but the World Church governs the entire world.

~

"What are you doing in the library at this hour, Henry?" a voice said, interrupting my workflow. It was Justin. Besides the occasional acquaintance from Jiu-Jitsu class, Justin was a close friend of mine since I'd started my last semester at The College. Mid-semester, Justin arrived at my History IV class. I was taking History IV again because I'd failed it the first go-around. I guess one could say it was History V for me. The only reason I noticed was because he was always accompanied by his girlfriend, the most beautiful woman I had ever seen, Anne-Marie. She was simple in beauty, but that made her stand out. I had never seen them around campus before my last semester. They both seemed to have appeared out of nowhere.

"You call this a library?" I asked. There were only two bookshelves along the center of the great room, which contained only 500 books. The pyramid-shaped room we referred to as our library was mostly filled with computers. There were so many computers in our library that the students eventually dubbed it Computer City. I remembered a time when a library, half the size of ours, had been filled with bookshelf after bookshelf, and there were only two computers in the entire library. One computer for students to use to look up information via the Network and the other for the librarian to use. Not too many people who used a library were interested in computers, let alone knew how to use them. Libraries were for books. Things changed.

Books were scarce these days because of computers. Not too many people liked the feel of books or the slow process it took to look through them. I had read every history book in the library since entering college, twice. That's how much I loved books. And history. Every now and then, I'd catch a glimpse or brief reference about the First World, or the High Universal Being, but they were only brief references that were cited as strictly fiction. Any mention of the First World or HUB was omitted, and it seemed to me like it was almost intentional. The only time I came across the brief mention of the Ventidos was in one of the five children's books we had in our so-called library, titled, *The Lost*

Legends and Other Scary Stories for Children. It wasn't even mentioned in the text.

If not for my appreciation of art, especially detailed drawings of ancient fictional creatures of old, I would have passed it by. The word was drawn in one of the illustrations that lined the book, and you had to be not only looking at the art but also really appreciating the fine details to have noticed it. Not to mention that it was written both upside down and backwards on the shadow from a cloak of one of the demon characters standing next to what could only be described as a pair of giant legs depicted in the drawing. I never cared for the picture, but since the book was over three hundred years old, and it was one of the five children's books in our library, I studied the picture despite myself.

I once asked our librarian, Ms. Snicth, about the purpose of the children's books in our library, and all she said was, "It's to open your mind to the world of children." Back then, I thought it was for the students studying to become a schoolteacher or something. I would eventually know better.

"I was trying to write a few more pages for my thesis," I replied. "Trying to get all of this information together and written down, so that it all makes sense, is taking me forever."

"Forever is worth writing about," Anne-Marie and Justin said at precisely the same time. They always did that. Repeating one another. They were meant to be, I thought.

"It's hard at times because nothing is really written down about the topic I am trying to research. I always end up at dead ends using the few books here, and when I try to access the Network, the trail ends in this vast library of books," I said sarcastically, my widespread arms gesturing toward the two bookshelves in the library. "I end up on Network Pages that only talk about conspiracy theories, which go around in circles, always back to the same thing about Sky Cameras, Poisonous Resources, Aliens, and Famous Suicides. It drives me crazy reading through all this useless information and trying to make any sense of it!" I said. "Even worse, some of the pages that seemed credible and provided most of the details for my research are now blocked, censored, or nonexistent."

"Strange," Justin said. "In the short time I have known you, you have always been obsessive about being right, even if it takes excessive research to prove so. The world needs more people like you, Henry. Hungry for understanding and eager to search it out."

Anne-Marie just nodded in agreement. She wasn't the outspoken type. *Justin is a lucky man*, I thought.

"You would think that I would be able to find more information for my thesis in the Encyclopedias we have or throughout the Network, but I have found more in the children's books that are here than in any Network Page or notable Encyclopedia," I said. "It doesn't feel right."

"One day it will all make sense, Henry," Justin said. "Take a break and let's get something to eat at the food hall."

I hadn't eaten all day, but that was nothing new. I was always broke and starving. I knew my thesis could open new doors for me. I did not know that it would change the world as we all knew it. I did not see the connections. I guess I was too hungry to notice.

I saved my progress to my computer card and gathered my things. Justin, Anne-Marie, and I left the library and went to the food hall.

~

"Try this apple, it's delicious," I said to the couple. We finished having fish and rice, and still hungry,

I grabbed from the last remaining fruits in the food hall at this hour. Only red apples were left.

"I would, but I know that Justin is allergic to apples of any kind," Anne-Marie said, "and besides, I would feel guilty after having one."

I shrugged and enjoyed my red apple anyway. While I ate the apple, Justin brought up an interesting point.

"Do you remember in the 1990s when almost every fruit had seeds?" Justin asked.

"I was born in '96, Justin. All I know is what my parents tell me: that in the 90s, the Establishment started marketing the value of having seedless fruits," I said. Everyone from Newtop Landmass believed that the Establishment had always governed with the best interests of the people in mind. Nothing could be further from the truth these days.

"They mentioned it was easier, faster to eat, and less of a nuisance. I really remember my parents always complaining that the cost of seedless fruits of any kind were pricier than the seeded kind," I added.

"Have you ever noticed that the price of seedless fruits is much cheaper than the fruits with seeds nowadays?" Justin asked.

"I've never paid attention. All I know is that I buy what I can afford. If it fits in my budget, then I try to appreciate it as I would if it were more expensive," I said to him.

"That's what I like about you, Henry," Justin said, as he slapped my back with enthusiasm. "You appreciate everything that you have, even if it isn't much."

I didn't know whether he was being condescending or trying to be encouraging, but I tried to brush it off. I never thought about the fact that most of the fruits I bought were lacking seeds. I never cared, mostly because I couldn't afford the higher priced fruits anyway. Being the type to have to understand why things are the way they are, I made a mental note to research the seedless fruits.

"How many seeds are in the core of your apple?" Justin asked.

I looked. "None."

Instantly my mind started turning, questioning why there are seedless fruits, how are they made, who makes them, what is the purpose of seeds, do seeds make a difference in the way an apple tastes, and so on and so on. I must have looked lost in thought because when Justin and Anne-Marie got up to clear their plates, I barely noticed that they had even left the table.

"We're gonna take off, Henry," Justin said, as he headed out of the food hall with Anne-Marie. "Seeds are mentioned in the Old Book!" he called out, as they rounded the corner. Anne-Marie simply waved good-bye.

~

According to the Old Book, it was said that "*...the apple was considered the blindfold fruit. HUB said it would blind many to the First World. A maker of giants, and one of the leaders of the Ventidos, tricked the first couple into taking their first bites of an apple. The woman bit first and the man took a bite shortly after. Only one bite and the entire world changed for the first couple. Instantly they were blind to the world they lived in. Their eyes were open to the new land around them. They now knew that the First World was full of peace and that the new land they now stood in was full of struggle. HUB gave the first couple the seeds to sow throughout the New World.*"

That's all that was mentioned.

"Well, that was interesting," I said out loud to myself. At the very most, I had found my second reference to the Ventidos. There had to be more information about them, but if not in the Old Book, then where? But who in the hell was this "maker of giants?" And how many were there? Giants, I knew for sure, were only written about in books like *Old Hendrix's Bedtime Stories*. With a sigh, I thought to myself, more research to do...

At the very least, the first chapter in the Old Book proved to be a good reference. I had many clues as to where to look next. I was supposed to be researching seeds, as Justin mentioned. He was a whole lot smarter than me, and I was grateful for the guidance. I had no idea why I chose to look in the Old Book as opposed to the Network first, but the fact that so many Network Pages were not trustworthy, and the Old Book has been around since the start of the written word, I figured I was bound to find something about seeds there. I was right. Justin was right.

But what did I know about apples? All I knew about apples was the children's rhyme that was recited during grade school.

An apple-a-day
Keeps the doctor away
But don't go eating the seeds
'Cause everyone knows
Eat too many of those
And they will be resting in peace

That was about it as far as apples. At any rate, I was tired of researching and writing. My next Jiu-Jitsu class was gonna begin in the next half-hour, and I was feeling content with my day's work. Knowing I was heading to study something a bit more fun, I smiled to myself as I put my research materials into my pack—Old Book rented from the library, grey ink pen, notepad, and computer card. Walking through the bookshelves to catch a whiff of the library books, as I always did leaving Computer City, I thought another happy thought: "I may be broke, but I will always have enough money for beer and Jiu-Jitsu!"

Chapter 2

Food Source Food Store, or FSFS for short, was the only organic food store on the campus. The rest of the stores were stocked with food provided from the Establishment. Although I worked there as a cook for the deli, I could not afford the food, even with my employee discount.

Hilo Eden, or just Hilo, as she preferred to be called, was the owner and operator of Food Source Food Store. When she wasn't running FSFS, she was providing Exercise Therapy sessions for her clients at the school gymnasium. She hired me last semester as a cook when the head cook quit due to a better job opportunity. Lucky for me because I was good at cooking and, to tell the truth, I really enjoyed it. Working at FSFS helped me to pay my rent, put myself through Jiu-Jitsu classes, and provided me with enough tip money to buy beer each day.

Hilo surprised me because she was only 23, a year or so younger than me, and yet she ran a very successful operation. Some rumors say she inherited it from her dad, and other rumors say it was a gift from her mom. It didn't matter. Hilo was young, she was beautiful, extremely smart, and she knew about nutrition and how to stay fit through a clean diet coupled with proper exercise. This was beneficial to her, especially in a time when the only other option for nutrition came from Establishment food, which everyone with a good head on their shoulders knew was bland, canned, and poorly fit to nourish one's body.

As I worked that rainy morning, marinating the chicken for the evening dinner rush, I reflected on how much I enjoyed cooking with the finest and freshest ingredients across the Seven Landmasses. I preferred the taste and the scent of the ingredients at FSFS. On the rare occasion I spent my money on groceries from FSFS instead of using that money for beer—which was usually before each Annual Interlandmass Jiu-Jitsu tournament—I realized that the foods from FSFS surpassed the quality and flavor of every other food that I had consumed and digested, sometimes with ill-effect, from B-mart, Brownwalls, and the rest of the affordable food markets stocked by the Establishment. Most of all, that rainy work morning, I finally became aware of how much I liked being around Hilo Eden.

All of my life I have been naturally fit, but when the motivation to train escaped me, Hilo Eden was a good excuse to frequent the gymnasium. I would train at the school gym just to watch her give Exercise Therapy lessons from a gym mirror across the room so she wouldn't see me looking. At first, I was watching to learn how to properly execute a squat, then I'd find myself watching her because she captured me with her every movement. Hilo was like a song that summoned tears, undiscovered love, and hidden emotions all at once. Poetry. She also attended my Jiu-Jitsu classes from time-to-time. She'd arm-barred me last night, and I was amazed.

The thought came to me like a flicker of light as I was putting the last tray of marinated chicken in the walk-in fridge. Hilo Eden would know more about seeds than anyone else on campus. The notion hadn't crossed my mind all semester, but maybe interviewing her for my thesis provided me with a good enough reason to finally go and talk to her. Girls like her were in short supply at The College—maybe the entire planet—and she was single as far as I knew. Interviewing her was a good opportunity to finally get to know Hilo on a more personal level.

"Hilo!" I called out, as she entered FSFS wearing black yoga pants and a white tank top, obviously returning from an Exercise Therapy session. "Can I talk to you?" I said eagerly. I was ashamed at how eager it sounded, but the ball started rolling as they say.

"Sure, Henry," she said, sounding winded. "That run up College Hill takes it out of me!" Her breath was labored but she managed to smile in-between breaths. "What'd you wanna talk about?"

"Seeds."

If I had been paying more attention to her words than I was to her natural beauty in yoga attire, and the way she glowed while she was sweaty, I would have noticed that she was suspiciously eyeing me when she responded with a question.

"Seeds?" she asked.

I didn't respond for who knows how long. She knew I wasn't paying attention to her words. I was only shaken out of my daydream of kissing her when she asked me a bit louder and on the verge of irritation, "Henry, why do you want to know about seeds?"

"Well, I figured you were the best person to ask since you run an all-natural health food store," I said sheepishly. She'd caught me looking. Worse things could have happened to me, I figured.

Hilo sighed but was too polite to show her disappointment. "We can talk when your shift ends. Sound good?"

I tried to keep my voice relaxed and my expression cool. "Where do you want to meet?" I said, praying I didn't sound too eager.

"Come up the winding staircase out back that leads to my loft above the food store."

"You live above FSFS?" I asked excitedly. All of my inhibitions were gone.

"Keep your voice down!" she ordered. "I don't want many customers to know where I live. Geez, Henry, haven't you heard of privacy?" she asked, as she headed down the Bath and Beauty aisle and out of sight.

"See you tonight!" I hollered with a smile as wide as the half moon. She'd already caught me staring at her. I didn't care if I sounded excited.

~

Her apartment loft was cozy and clean. She wasn't the kind to clutter. A Far East style decorated her apartment loft in an elegant, functional, and simple manner. It figures, I thought. She was not only focused in her professions, but judging Hilo by her living standard, she was organized in mind, body, spirit, and in lifestyle.

The windows were made of seven-layered rice paper but allowed just enough sunlight and outside air to enter the room. It felt like I was on the beach and behind a waterfall at the same time. Her house smelled of roses and fresh rain—probably because of the fresh flowers of every vibrant color, which decorated the shelf that lined her kitchen sink. I could hear the ocean waves in the background and wondered where the ambient noise was coming from, but I stopped wondering when she sat down next to me on the oat-colored futon, handing me a cup of Jasmine tea and placing another hot cup in her lap. The sun was beginning to set, letting in the warm glow of pink, orange, and yellow colors. I was more than grateful to be next to Hilo.

"Robert Fencewood, the billionaire inventor of Chiptech software, bought up all of the seeds across the Seven Landmasses and stores them on the coldest Island Landmass—which some say he also owns—in an underground, multilevel facility only a handful of people know about," Hilo said. "According to a few encrypted sites that release both restricted and classified information on the

Network, known as Shadow Pages, Fencewood's top secret facility, where studies and experiments are conducted on every kind of remaining seed, is officially called Nutrisource. In underground terminology, it's simply known as the Source."

I scribbled down notes in my notepad as quickly and legibly as possible. To say that my mind was racing with question after question so I could gather enough research for my thesis paper and conclude the interview with Hilo would be a lie. Truth be told, I was just thinking about how it would feel to kiss Hilo. Even if I wanted to, I couldn't find a way to keep the conversation going on any longer. Long story short, when she looked at me, all I did was smile and take another sip of tea.

Not knowing what to say, I awkwardly smiled at her. Then my eyes wandered, and I noticed the Old Book that was leaning against the hundreds of books that filled her small library. I set my cup of tea down on a small Far Eastern tea table. The bookshelf looked expensive, but I could tell it was handmade. Nonetheless it was made extremely sturdy and out of bamboo and bramble berry wood and stretched all along the back wall of her small apartment loft—just below Hilo's bedroom. It was light and sturdy, and the color of a cold beer outlined with a dark mocha. She possessed books of all ages. I recognized a few of the books that filled her personal library, but she had hundreds of books I had never even seen before.

"Mind if I look at your library?" I asked, not worried that my curiosity had gotten the best of me.

"Be my guest," Hilo said.

I got up and walked over to the shelves that stood on the wall opposite of the rice paper windows, just below her bedroom. I must have looked through her library for what seemed to be an eternity. Hilo made a batch of fresh tea in the kitchen while I was indulging myself in her bookcases. Not recognizing many of the books by their titles or material, and reluctant to overstay my welcome, I grabbed the one book I was familiar with, her copy of the Old Book, and returned to sit next to Hilo on the futon. It felt thicker and heavier than any other Old Book I had ever seen.

"Your Old Book is different," I stated, while looking over the book. I opened the pages and noticed a smell of old leather and cinnamon, a spice not common to our Landmass.

"That's because it is," Hilo said matter-of-factly. "It came from Ethipon. My dad gave it to me."

"Is that in Middle East Landmass?" I asked.

"It's in Oldland. Ethipon is known for having the most accurate copies of the Old Book," she explained. "It's close to where the famous Stone Triangle Temples of antiquity are. My parents believed that the location where the First Couple were banished out of the First World was located somewhere near Ethipon," Hilo said, before she took a couple more sips of her tea.

"Where'd you get all of these books?" I asked, gesturing towards her collection, while holding the heavier copy of the Old Book in hand.

"My dad was a book collector for a secret acquisitions unit of the World Church for most of his professional career. He would bring home books he thought were interesting. I didn't know he was pilfering books out of the World Church's library at the time," Hilo said. With a look of longing, she added, "One day my dad brought home that copy of the Old Book. I remember my parents were really excited about it. He returned to work the next day, and I haven't seen him since."

I could tell she missed her dad. To say missed was an understatement. She loved her dad very much. She had kept many pictures in between the spaces of books in her library shelves of her with her mom and dad. But mostly pictures of her with her dad. Hoping to change the subject, I asked about her mom.

"How's your mom doing these days?" I asked and then instantly regretted it.

"My mom was a farmer who practiced and kept ancient knowledge of gardening and holistic healing passed down for centuries from generation to generation. She came from a family line of Native Healers from Newtop Landmass that kept no written record. Everything they knew was passed down to their children to keep the information secret. My mom was *killed* because she wrote down the healing traditions in a book, no matter what any report says." Hilo was on the verge of tears. There were no other family pictures in her house.

I sat silently, not knowing what to say. I'd screwed up twice already.

Luckily, Hilo filled the silence. "It was forbidden to write down the Knowledge of Seeds, as my mom called it, but not because it was sacred. It was forbidden to write down our traditions because if that kind of knowledge fell into the wrong hands, the remedies would be studied and eventually only used for profit by some Establishment in one way or another. Even worse, if any mad scientist got ahold of the natural remedies, they could end up genetically altering the healing properties that cure diseases out of the many different plants or fruits or vegetables or spices listed in the book. Healing properties would then be altered for every generation that follows. Seeds that grow food without nutrients are useless. Do you understand, Henry?"

We sat in silence for a few minutes and drank more tea. Hilo was lost in her memories while I was lost in thought, caught up by the flood of information.

"I'd better get going," I said, not wanting to make Hilo cry or dig myself deeper into the friend zone. "Thanks for everything, Hilo," I said. "I'll see you at work or hopefully tomorrow night at Jiu-Jitsu."

"I enjoyed it, Henry. You're more than welcome to pick my brain or go through my books at any time," Hilo said. She got up to go to her kitchen and returned within a few minutes with a sealed brown envelope in hand.

Before I could ask, Hilo handed me the brown envelope, still blinking away any sign of tears, and with a sly smile said, "I may stop in Jiu-Jitsu class tomorrow night to beat you around a little."

I don't know why at the time—it could have been because of her apartment decor—but I stood up and bowed in appreciation, as they do in the Far East Landmass. No expression on my face. Hilo let out a laugh at the gesture. "You're silly, Henry. I'm not Far Eastern," Hilo joked.

I finished my third glass of tea and gathered my notepad and pen and put them, along with the brown envelope, into my pack. I was heading out the door and about to say good-bye when Hilo called out, "Hey, Henry, wait a minute!" She ran back towards her bookshelf and hurriedly located two books that were on opposite ends of her bookshelf. She jogged up to me, and her hair slipped a little out of her ponytail. She handed me two ancient books by the look of them. They were both bound in dark leather and looked older than the copy of the Old Book she had. The Book of Enek and The Book of Yasr.

"Take these and use them for your thesis. They were removed from the Old Book before the World Church started the Holy Campaign that eventually led to the Many Agreements. I know you'll find them interesting. Bring them back when you find what you need," Hilo said, with a contented smile.

"Thanks, Hilo!" I said, while trying not to trip down the wooden stairs that led me out of Hilo's loft and into a moonlit alley behind FSFS. I carried the two books with me down to the alley before I decided to put them in my pack. When I opened my pack to put the two ancient books in, a small piece of paper, serving as a bookmark, fell to the street. I snatched the paper up and before putting it back in the book, I decided to read it. On the front it had Mr. Eden's name and mailing address. I was about to toss it in one of the many trash cans that was in the alley behind FSFS before I noticed there was more writing on the back. My eyes grew wide as I silently read Mr. Eden's handwriting. I had found my third reference about the Ventidos.

When the light flickers twice
And the crickets aren't chirping
When in an instant you go from fine to cold
When there are shadows all about
After the lights go out Ventidos

—Ethipon legend passed down from the
    First People once they were in the New Land

The bookmark spooked me, but I didn't let it ruin my night. I placed it back into one of the ancient books in my pack and decided to look inside of the brown envelope. The contents surprised me even more than the words on the back of Mr. Eden's makeshift bookmark. I opened the envelope and found a spare key to Hilo's loft along with a note. I walked home with high spirits, thankful because the note said I was *welcome to do research in Hilo's library between the hours of sunset to midnight during the weekends, and sunset to Jiu-Jitsu class during the week.*

I was so excited that night, I decided to read through The Book of Yasr in its entirety as soon as I reached my studio apartment above the local coffee shop, Rocky's Coffee. What I learned put the Old Book into greater perspective. I knew the reason for the Great Drowning. I knew why it had been removed from the Old Book.

I also knew where to look for more information about the Ventidos.

Chapter 3

The excitement from the time I'd spent with Hilo the night before, and the new knowledge of the Great Drowning, made it hard for me to sleep. The smell of freshly roasted coffee from below my apartment was enough to drive away any leftover drowsiness. I jumped out of bed and threw on some clothes before running downstairs to grab some coffee. Besides Jiu-Jitsu and beer, I could always afford a fresh cup of coffee. Rocky, the owner, usually gave me one free cup a day. I figured since he owned the shop and the studio apartment above, he just fixed the price of every cup of coffee that he had given me in with my total rent.

With the semester almost over and graduation nearing, I had to get to work on finishing my thesis so I could get it published. I was also scheduled to visit my parents for Midterm Break.

I reached the library before the yellow sun rose that warm spring morning. The singing birds were happy, and so was I. Ms. Snicth wasn't happy to see me waiting at the library doors before it opened. She rolled her eyes as she approached the double-doors, and I swear the birds stopped chirping. I smiled and sipped my coffee while she opened the doors to the library. From the entrance, it looked like all of the computer monitors were staring in reverence at the bookshelves by the way they were positioned, with glowing red eyes. They reminded me of the Monolithic Stone Heads of the outer Island Landmasses by the way they cascaded down from the peak of the triangle-shaped room up to the entrance. But instead of worshipping the sunrise like the Stone Heads, they worshipped the books. I could imagine from above the library it would resemble one big, red triangle eye by the way the library was assembled.

"Not enough booze and no one else to bug," she snapped, as she turned on the power source that lit up Computer City with enough light to blind the sun.

I would have responded, but I'd learned it was better to ignore a fool. Even if that fool were beautiful. Before sitting down to type at one of the many vacant computers in Computer City that early morning, thoughts ran through my mind that Ms. Snicth could use a boyfriend, or a hobby, or a puppy, or something that would bring a damn smile to her face. I remembered a time when libraries and librarians used to be warm and inviting. I brushed both her comment and my wandering thoughts off. I was the only one in Computer City from the time it opened and, since most college students in my day slept half of the day away, I knew I would be the only one there right up to lunchtime. Had it not been for my productive night with Hilo, I would probably still be sleeping, too, I thought, as I sipped my cup of Rocky's Coffee.

With the exception of the Shadow Pages on the Network, Computer City was useless to me. I did not even know how to get past the encrypted data to access the classified information anyway. If Hilo had not given me so many pointers to work with, I would probably be lost looking through Network pages that were either overly biased and unreliable or Network pages that were completely filled with outlandish conspiracy theories.

I looked up Robert Fencewood and only came up with his many works of philanthropy across the Seven Landmasses. I didn't know what was worse, being stuck with dead ends or being stuck rereading the same-old 500 books in the library at The College, searching for clues that I already knew weren't there. I thought, I could always go to Hilo's library, but I knew today I had to use my time and research wisely. Plus, I had to get my scattered notes from last night's interview with Hilo, and the many other thoughts that raced through my mind from our discussion, written down properly so I could think straight for the rest of the day and especially at tonight's Jiu-Jitsu class.

Before I started typing, I sat down to read through my notes and organize them mentally.

"If you're not here to use the computer or check out a library book, why did you come so early, Henry?" Ms. Snicth asked, breaking my concentration.

"I just wanted to keep you company, Ms. Snicth," I said, half-earnestly and half-sarcastically, hoping she wouldn't be able to tell the difference. "Every great author has to gather their thoughts before writing," I followed-up with a smile that would irritate an old wound.

She gasped in disbelief. "You're writing a book?"

"This book is going to change the world," I said matter-of-factly. "It's almost as important as the Old Book itself."

With that remark, Ms. Snicth raised an eyebrow. "Be careful, Henry," she said. "You could be swimming in deep waters, and you don't want to know what lurks in those waters." It sounded like a threat.

I waited to respond. My pride was in check, being that I trained a lot of Jiu-Jitsu. I remembered our motto, "Leave the ego at the door," as being a solid foundational belief that was practiced and preached throughout every Jiu-Jitsu Academy across the Seven Landmasses. I responded to her perceived threat with absolute humility and extreme confidence when I said, "A shark out of water is a lion on land."

I was never good with speaking, although it made more sense in my mind at the time. Even still, I was satisfied with my response and was about to go back to my research when I noticed Ms. Snicth discreetly grabbing her pocket phone from her purse. She hadn't taken her suspicious eyes off of me since my response, and was trying to secretly type a thumb message on her pocket phone, when the lights in Computer City flickered a few times, maybe only twice, but they flickered. It was then that I noticed it was a bit cooler in the library that morning. She just smiled at me shortly after. I felt uneasy.

Suddenly I heard footsteps. Mr. Beandrop, The College's History instructor, emerged from the staircase that led to the teacher's lounge that was beneath Computer City. It was no secret that underneath The College was a passageway of tunnels that connected every department building on campus to the teacher's lounge. Only teachers had access to the tunnels. Probably to access the staff bathrooms quicker.

Mr. Beandrop was followed up the stairs by my Jiu-Jitsu Professor, the renowned Professor U. Professor U. preferred to keep his full name private because many students have mispronounced his name over the years. Most of the time we just simply called him, Professor—as all black belts in Jiu-Jitsu are called. They were soon followed by my outdoor Survival Instructor, Mr. Freewheel. They were all carrying fresh cups of coffee, and with the exception of the Professor, they were eating chocolate donuts. Naturally, Mr. Beandrop had two donuts in hand.

Mr. Beandrop was a true scholar when it came to history and a true gentleman with the ladies to the point that it weirded them out. He was a cheerful man, but to some people, like Ms. Snicth, he was almost too nice and too eager to please, even if he meant no harm by it. Throughout my years at

The College, I learned what *not* to do with women by watching Mr. Beandrop interact with them. He loved visiting the library to read and was often seen amongst students using one of the many computers in Computer City. It was falsely rumored that there was something going on between him and Ms. Snicth, even though there was an apparent age difference of at least ten years between them.

As Mr. Beandrop approached, I was looking at Ms. Snicth more closely and took notice of her shoulder-length brown hair, glasses, green eyes, and tan skin that was found common to the people from the Newbottom Landmass. If it weren't for her attitude, I could see how she could actually be considered beautiful. I could also see how Mr. Beandrop's personality could actually balance hers. I wasn't surprised at all when he walked up to Ms. Snicth to hand her a chocolate donut.

"It was said that donuts kept the People of Hub alive in the desert during the Exodus of Oldland, and you, Ms. Snicth, have the look of a woman in need of a donut this morning. Without further adieu, I've come to save your life," Mr. Beandrop cheerfully said, as he placed the donut on top of Ms. Snicth's desk. His awkward way of communicating only seemed to push Ms. Snicth further away.

"Take your chocolate donut history and shove it down your bean hole, Beandrop! You know I am on a strict diet and exercise program," Ms. Snicth said, while looking at Mr. Beandrop like he was stupid. Every male student knew Ms. Snicth didn't have a bad figure, and it looked like she took exercise and diet seriously. She was fit for being in her mid-thirties.

Professor U. and Mr. Freewheel started laughing as they walked toward my direction. "Yin and Yang!" shouted Mr. Freewheel, as he looked at me and gestured with a thumb pointing back at Mr. Beandrop and Ms. Snicth. Mr. Freewheel wasn't afraid to speak his mind. He was the head instructor for the Survival Courses at The College, and he'd served in both the War of Towersfell and the controversial, almost never-ending War of the Far East. He was no one to trifle with, and the many medals of honor and certificates of merit in his office proved it. Not only that, he was the head instructor to the elite Collective Newtop Military Combatives Program. Nobody knows why he left the Newtop Military to become an instructor at The College. All I know is that I enjoyed Mr. Freewheel's classes because he taught how to strike hard, and, more importantly, where to strike first.

Besides hand-to-hand combat, he also taught us how to properly and safely use firearms. He began every class each day by saying, "This shit could save your ass!" He had a no bullshit approach to teaching, and he was never short of something offensive to say. Students either loved him or hated him, and most would drop out of his class after the first few weeks—mostly because of Mr. Freewheel's offensive language and military tone. It was his way or the highway, and if we screwed up, according to Mr. Freewheel, "You'll pay with your asses in one way or another." Mr. Freewheel was as tough as they come, but I could tell that he really wanted to inspire the next generation.

Ms. Snicth gave Mr. Freewheel a look of disapproval and threw her donut at the back of his head. Only she had the power to knock Mr. Freewheel down a couple of notches with just a look and a chocolate donut.

Mr. Freewheel picked the donut up off the floor, saluted Ms. Snicth, and ate it as he walked out of the library. Professor U. laughed even harder. I couldn't help but feel embarrassed for both Mr. Beandrop and Mr. Freewheel. I also couldn't help but bust out laughing at the recent events of the morning.

"He would have fit in well five hundred years ago with the Shupow Warriors of the Far East," Professor U. stated, as he walked up to me to shake my hand. "Are you coming to class tonight, Henry?"

"Yes indeed, Professor," I said.

The professor was the kind of person to use very few words, and it rubbed off on me when he was around. He simply nodded and headed to the library exit. Before exiting, he stopped, turned to look at Mr. Beandrop and Ms. Snicth, then back at me, and started to laugh as he walked away. I didn't know what to make of it and decided it was time to start adding what I had learned from Hilo and The Book of Yasr to my thesis.

~

Henry Gomez Thesis

Long before the Many Agreements, an aggressive acquisitions unit of the World Church began gathering ancient artifacts in order to confuse the world and hide the truth about our human origins. During this Holy Campaign, as it was referred to amongst a secret group of church members, the World Church was able to fill their underground library with thousands of sacred texts from antiquity, which contained sacred knowledge gathered from all across the Seven Landmasses. For hundreds of centuries that sacred knowledge, known as The Forbidden Fruits, was kept hidden away from the public. This eventually led to the intentional modification of the Old Book and the manipulation of the New World. With the Old Book altered, the World Church was able to rise above the Establishment that governed the people and rule the world.

Of all the texts gathered from the Holy Campaign, two religious texts were considered the most prized and were removed from the Old Book. The Book of Enek and The Book of Yasr were the names of the two books that were intentionally removed. They described, in great detail, the many parts of the Old Book that were hard to understand and difficult to explain with scientific study alone. For instance, the Great Drowning.

Scientific data all around the world could explain that there was indeed a great downpour, known as the Great Drowning in the Old Book, but no one knew the reason why the Great Drowning occurred. According to the Book of Yasr, the world was flooded to kill off both the corrupt and the mixed species. Unguided by Enek, the teacher of angels, who found favor with HUB and was the first man accepted into the First World without dying, the new people of the new land turned to evil ways and corrupted the New World. HUB punished them by rendering their *seeds useless. They reaped only thorns no matter what they sowed. In great anger, the new people laid waste to each other, robbed and raped each other, and, worst of all, they began mixing one species with another. The genetic code was altered, and hybrids roamed the world. All men and all animals were corrupted. With great anger, HUB cleansed the planet from all corruption of the flesh with the Great Drowning.*

~

It took nearly two-and-a-half hours to organize my notes and type what I had learned from last night's interview with Hilo and The Book of Yasr so it made sense. I also realized that the whole time I'd been working on my thesis, I'd neglected my half-filled cup of Rocky's Coffee. I downed my coffee, which was still robust and flavorful considering it was cold at that point, and decided it was wise to save my progress to my computer card. In all of my years, I knew that if I lost all of my progress up to that point, I would rather fail History IV again and spend the rest of the semester drinking beer alone at Tivoli Tavern.

I had just saved my progress and removed my computer card from the computer right when the power in Computer City shut down. I was relieved

I had all my hard work safely in hand. There were times when I had lost all my data during power outages, even if they were as rare as being struck by lightning. At any rate, I felt like I had just been struck by lightning and decided to start gathering my notepad and computer card into my pack as Ms. Snicth reset the breakers below Computer City and restored the power. I was about to log out of my computer when I heard Justin's voice.

"You look like you could use a fresh cup of Rocky's Coffee," he said, as he sat down next to me. Anne-Marie stood expressionless at his side carrying a to-go box full of Rocky's Coffee.

"You read my mind," I said with a smile, as I logged out of my computer and grabbed my cup to get a refill of the fresh coffee. I happily extended my empty cup to Anne-Marie and was pleased that she didn't spill a drop while refilling my coffee.

"Almost done with your thesis?" Justin asked.

"Not yet," I said. "I still have so far to go, but the good news is I have found a few more leads from an unexpected resource."

"Is that so," Justin said, as he crossed his arms then asked, "May I read what you have written so far?"

I was a little reluctant to put my computer card back into any computer that day for fear of losing more progress from another unexpected power outage. But the truth was I really wanted a beer to drink and something to eat. Not to mention, I couldn't figure out the meaning behind Justin's defensive posture and eagerness to read about what I had written. Yet he was still my closest friend, and I wanted to get away from the library and all the computers.

"Tell you what," I said, before taking a sip of Rocky's Coffee, "I'll tell you all about it at Tivoli Tavern."

"Deal!" Justin said.

~

I was promoted to black belt in Jiu-Jitsu that night. It had taken me a little over ten years of consistent study in the ancient art to finally reach my goal of becoming a Professor. I felt like crying tears of joy, but Hilo was in attendance at Jiu-Jitsu class that night. Real men do cry, but when she was present, I couldn't muster up the strength to do so. She was powerful and beautiful, and I planned to kiss her first before I ever shed a tear in front of her. Besides that, she submitted me with a gnarly triangle choke during training that night and my pride, though in check, was still a little sore.

All-in-all, it had been a good day.

Chapter 4

I was waiting with my fully-loaded assault rife in arms dressed in Newtop Military fatigues, along with the rest of the seven armed members of Mr. Freewheel's class, for the Outdoor Assault lesson to begin. As always, Mr. Freewheel paced in front of us at the front of the room, back and forth militarily, while deciding what to say to start the lesson for the day. It wasn't that he was unorganized or that he was a poor planner. Mr. Freewheel was as methodical as a pack of wolves. He was never late and was often found sitting silently at his desk before the morning roosters crowed or any of his classes began, holding his coffee mug and staring intently into space. He looked like a lion about to pounce, or a king who was mentally deciding the best plan of action to use to win a war. Though most of his instruction was taught in the Battle Rooms located in the jungles outside of campus, every lesson began in room 144-000, the Hand-to-Hand Combat room of the Survival Studies Department Building at The College.

Mr. Freewheel looked like he was having a conversation with himself, although his lips were sealed shut. He only nodded slowly in response to whatever conversation was going on in his head. He was staring at something we couldn't see, and no one, with any sense left in them, ever bothered to shake him out of his daydream. We just stood at attention until Mr. Freewheel was ready.

He couldn't have been older than 37, but he walked with the confidence of knowing that he had seen things no one else had seen and done things no one else had done. Real things. He had the wisdom of a man twice his age.

He was dressed in black from head-to-toe. He was wearing a black beret and had an assault rifle slung down and across his back. Mr. Freewheel was completely bald. It didn't matter. Mr. Freewheel had a strong look about him with his square jaw, lined with 5 o'clock shadow, thick black eyebrows, and blue eyes that always seemed to be saying, "I am not the one to fuck with."

Part 1

"Our orders are to recover the rest of the Advanced Special Operations Unit, which went missing during a classified reconnaissance mission roughly fifty-five miles from our twenty. Five members are still missing from Team 1, and we're gonna find them and bring them home!" said the female Task Unit Commander, almost yelling to be heard over the spinning blades and roaring engines of the Warchopper that was on the flight deck of the Newtop Military Water Vessel, the Sea Eagle.

The vessel was anchored at the edge of the world. It was swaying aggressively from the rough waters that pounded, with the force and sound of atoms splitting, up against the massive landmass known only as the Arctic Ring of Frozen Waters. The Arctic Ring of Frozen Waters, or simply Frozen Waters for short amongst the Newtop armed forces, stood three miles above sea level and completely surrounded the Seven Landmasses. No citizen from any state, from any of the Seven Landmasses, was allowed to visit the Frozen Waters. The Establishment of every Landmass had a treaty in place that only allowed authorized military personnel to visit the top secret location.

All Freewheel knew about their location was that he was south of the Newbottom Landmass. The only thought that ran through his mind while the commander spoke was that he was about to get into some crazy shit. If Team 1, the baddest of the badasses, suffered and lost greatly in the unexplored region, their unit was gonna have one hell of a time.

Freewheel listened along with the rest of his Advanced Special Operations Unit, referred to as Team 2. The eight-man unit of Team 2 waited outside, unaffected by the cold wind and turbulence stirring all around the Water Vessel, awaiting further instructions from the Task Unit Commander before they filed into the Warchopper.

. . .

"Most people would agree that the history of your name, Freewheel, is a combination of the words Free and Will. But did you know that Free Will was a gift?" the Medic/Navigator of Team 2 asked, an hour into the bumpy flight.

"Save it, Pastor," Freewheel said to the Medic/Navigator. The Medic/Navigator was known as Pastor amongst the unit because he was always talking about The Savior and the One Agreement of the Old Book. Not a mission went by when he didn't try to let the other members in on his beliefs.

The Medic/Navigator continued. "It was the greatest gift of all because, although HUB created us, we were given the option to make our own decisions. Meaning we could create our own lives, even if all of our destinies were already written. Here's the kicker, Freewheel," the Medic/Navigator happily carried on. "Everyone has the gift of Free Will, even if they choose to believe in HUB or not."

"Quit tryin' to save my soul. Pastor. I don't have one," Freewheel said and then started to load another clip with bullets.

"Not true, Freewheel. We all have a soul, and it can be saved only by The Savior. The only ones without souls are the red-headed giants."

"Here we go again with that giant shit!" Freewheel said, throwing his hands up, apparently annoyed.

"It's true," the Medic/Navigator said matter-of-factly. "The red-headed giants weren't created by HUB, and when they died during the Great Drowning, they became demons. Besides, everyone has heard the joke that 'red heads have no souls' at one time or another. But only a handful of people actually know the origins of the joke."

Freewheel tried to ignore the Medic/Navigator but found that he couldn't stop listening and, even worse, he was pondering the words he'd said. The Medic/Navigator knew he was getting somewhere with Freewheel for the first time and decided to say, "All of HUB's creations have a soul, even you, Freewheel."

"Pastor, another damn word out of you, and I will bleed you right here, right now!" Freewheel spat.

The Medic/Navigator smiled patiently, understanding that he had pushed his limits with Freewheel that day with ancient history. No one read as much as the Medic/Navigator and, even if they did read, no one cared to read the kinds of books the Medic/Navigator enjoyed. He had read the Book of Enek, a holy book known to only a handful of people, and he knew about red-headed giants and their origins. He knew the Sinpaz created the great giants. He knew the giants were only ever mentioned in books like *Old Hendrix's Bedtime Stories* to cover up their authenticity. He knew HUB had drowned the 200 members, known as the Sinpaz, along with the rest of the world, and imprisoned their 22 leaders in the region known as the Frozen Waters. He was the only member of Team 2 who wasn't surprised when the real rescue mission began. He was the only one with a cool head on his shoulders when all hell broke loose.

. . .

The Warchopper started its descent into a huge hole that was in the Frozen Waters, like a speck of dust falling into the abyss. The hole was big enough to fit a small island landmass inside. Team 2 gathered their rifles and rucksacks after the Warchopper landed. The Medic/Navigator was the first to jump out of the Warchopper that landed closer to the southernmost side of the giant hole, followed shortly after by the rest of the unit members of Team 2.

Team 2 was surrounded by numerous tunnels that seemed to extend forever. They were vast and extended in every direction from the center of the huge hole. It was easy to get lost. The tunnels weren't blue, they weren't white, and they weren't grey. The tunnels were a mixture between all three of the colors. Freewheel thought to himself that if he were stuck inside of an ice cube, and he were asked to describe the color, that would be the best description of the place where the team stood. The landscape looked alien. Besides having an indescribable color, it was damn cold. A cold wind was constantly blowing throughout the tunnels that cut through their specialized uniforms, which were meant to withstand minus 235 degrees Celsius, and Freewheel wondered where it was coming from.

There were gigantic, glowing symbols, which resembled both hieroglyphs and runes, drawn along the sides of each tunnel's entrance. It looked to Freewheel like a spell was written along each of the tunnel walls. He thought he could hear whispers carried by the cold wind.

Team 2 stood by the Warchopper with rifles pointed in each direction, at the ready, waiting for the Medic/Navigator to lead the way. The Medic/Navigator signaled for the team to wait there, grabbed a book from his white camouflaged rucksack, and began flipping through it. The book looked ancient from what Freewheel could tell, and the Medic/Navigator was obviously reading a map. The outside of the map was lined with ancient writing, but Freewheel could barely see the details from where he stood. The Medic/Navigator put his book away, then ran up to one of the tunnel entrances a hundred yards ahead of the team. He walked up to one of the large tunnel walls and inspected the alien writing that was etched into the ice. After a few minutes, the Medic/Navigator gave the signal for the group to join him. The rest of Team 2 ran up behind him, settled into battle formation, and started slowly down the huge, frozen tunnel.

They reached the downed Warchopper of Team 1 about an hour into their trek. It looked like it had been torn to pieces and scattered all around the frozen cavern as far as the eye could see. There was debris everywhere, and the tunnel smelled of rotting flesh and burnt garbage. The team walked up to what had to be the remains of the rest of the five members of Advanced Special Operations Unit Team 1, their broken equipment, and torn-apart Warchopper. One of the men looked like he had been bitten in half. All that was left was the bottom of his legs. What could only be described as teeth marks lined the body of one of the men, and descended all the way down from what the team could make of his head, to the remaining parts of his torso and right leg, looking the way a bite mark looks on a piece of bread. They could barely recognize the rest of the unit. The remains looked like they had been gnawed on, and there was no flesh on the bones. Everything was simmering in small flames surrounding the area.

Minutes later, a roar shook the entire cavern.

"FIRE!" screamed the Task Unit Commander of Team 2. Freewheel stood motionless for what felt like an eternity, staring at the sight. A massive being, which could only be described as a giant, entered the cavern from one of the tunnels and attacked the unit. The Pastor was the first to open fire on the beast with heavy artillery, launching grenades at the creature's head from his grenade launcher, but only hitting its belly. Explosions rattled the cave. The giant, irritated and angrier, was moving quicker towards one of the unit members of Team 2. Freewheel saw its red hair toss wildly in the cavern as the giant turned, then thrust a huge spear made from the blade of Team 1's Warchopper with great speed and deadly accuracy through one of Team 2's members who flanked the giant's right side. He was still firing up at the giant's face before he passed.

At the sight, Freewheel finally joined in the battle. He grabbed his rocket-propelled grenade launcher. He aimed and released a rocket at the giant's right knee. The giant fell to one knee and threw the spear, which still held the lanced member of Team 2, towards Freewheel's direction. It stuck hard into the icy cavern wall. The giant screamed in anger, having missed his target. It was trying to recklessly grab at the rest of Team 2 with swiping motions of his giant arms while being peppered with a barrage of ammo. Closer in range, the rest of Team 2 unleashed their entire arsenal upon the giant. They dumped their entire payload, unloading every bullet from every rifle and launching every explosive they had directly at the giant's head. It took all of their firepower to finally kill the giant. It looked like the apocalypse had occurred in the icy cavern.

The Task Unit Commander from Team 2 radioed-in the report to the Newtop Military Command Center shortly after the unbelievable battle. Her instructions were clear. Team 2 was ordered to remain silent about the mission. Furthermore, they were not allowed to ask about the three surviving members of Team 1.

A while later, their Warchopper arrived in the war-torn cavern. Team 2, along with Team 1's remains and the fallen giant, were picked up out of the cavern and flown back to the Sea Eagle. The giant was secured with specialized military-grade straps and a massive, heavy-duty harness designed to haul extremely large items. Fifty tons of bundled-up giant dangled from the huge harness at the bottom of the Warchopper, as it made its ascent rising from the frozen abyss, literally carrying dead weight. Every member of Advanced Special Operations Unit Team 2 remained silent the entire way back to base. It was a slow flight out of the Frozen Waters.

• • •

From one of the windows, Freewheel thought he spotted something flying out of the waters near the Water Vessel. It defied any laws of flight by the way it maneuvered around the Warchopper. At light speed, it flew back into the water. Freewheel decided to keep that to himself.

• • •

Back on the Newtop Military Water Vessel, the *Sea Eagle*, the members of Advanced Special Operations Unit Team 2 were debriefed one-by-one. Freewheel and the Medic/Navigator were the last two members who waited to debrief. The Chief Newtop Military Commander summoned Freewheel into his office. Freewheel got up and walked up to the Chief Commander's doorway, turned to the Medic/

Navigator, and said, "I'd like to know more about salvation, Pastor Eden."

Part 2

The flight to Jyberjab would have been considered smooth and uneventful, thought Task Unit 3 Commander Freewheel, as he sipped on a glass of whiskey, had it not been for the assassination that was broadcast over the military monitors. He watched in utter disbelief the breaking news coverage. Advanced Special Operations Unit Team 3, Freewheel's new unit with new team members, watched alongside him.

"The President of Newtop Landmass, Geo J. Weatherbee, was killed in broad daylight, as his motorcade was on its way to meet with a few other Newtop state leaders to discuss his reelection that summer," said the broadcaster. "President Geo J. Weatherbee was heading to discuss the slow and steady implementation of any new, controversial technologies. He hoped to discuss better ways to keep things transparent with the public, especially regarding changes in currency and health practices.

He believed that man was more valuable than any machine and encouraged reading for every citizen, regarding books as an essential resource. He stood firmly against genetic modification, otherwise known as gene therapy, and was considered vocal, given political restraints on topics pertaining to The Savior," added the broadcaster. "He is survived by his wife and two children. Newtop Landmass has taken a massive blow today."

Freewheel sipped more whiskey, speechless. In a short moment, more sad news was transmitted over the military monitor.

"We interrupt this broadcast and regret to reveal more breaking news. Towersfell, the World Economic Center of Commerce, has been demolished by what can only be described as unknown Jyberi extremists." The broadcaster continued. "It is a sad day for Newtop Landmass, and the Vice President has declared war against all of Jyberjab and the Jyberi extremists."

Photos of the extremists were displayed over the broadcast, while the Vice President said, "We stand against extremists and will punish those responsible for the destruction. We will hold them accountable to the full extent of United Landmass

Law. We will find their weapons of destruction and destroy them."

Freewheel couldn't tell whether the "them" to which the Vice President was referring was the Jyberi nation or the weapons.

Commander Freewheel got up at the end of the broadcast to grab the whole bottle of whiskey. He filled his glass and watched the assassination in slow motion, playing back the broadcast on the military monitor. He recognized the plot immediately. After all, he had taught it to the group of highly trained Secret Intelligence Officers who had pulled it off. He knew the name of the limo driver who had shot the President while no one else noticed.

It was smooth and calculated. Other shots were fired from the crowd as a diversion. Onlookers were screaming in disarray. Only a trained eye could see the gunman turn briefly while driving, and, with his left hand point the silver handgun over his right shoulder. He pulled off the professional hit, putting a bullet through the head of Newtop Landmass' favorite President. He knew the Intelligence Officers involved would get away unscathed. Freewheel also knew the Jyberi men who were supposedly held responsible for the destruction of

Towersfell. He knew very well they weren't the only extremists involved. They were working alongside Special Operations Units within the Secret Intelligence Agency on a secret project to restore Middle East relations with Newtop Landmass. He knew all of this because he had trained each and every one of them as well.

Freewheel knew he was involved in both the assassination and destruction of Towersfell in one way or another. He'd inadvertently helped replace the best President in all of Newtop history and also helped start a new war in a single day.

Task Unit Commander Freewheel downed the glass of whiskey and began drinking from the bottle as he stared out of the Warchopper heading to the Middle East. He created his letter of resignation during the rest of the flight to Jyberjab.

. . .

Pastor Eden ran into Freewheel at the Newtop Base located in the middle of the Jyberjab desert.

"Pastor, it's good to see you, you son of a bitch!"

"Likewise, Freewheel. It's been too long!" The two former members of Advanced Special Operations

Unit Team 2 shook hands firmly while the sun was coming up over the horizon.

"I'm here with my team on a mission to investigate weapons of mass destruction," Freewheel said. "Got any leads?"

"Remember the Tower of Jyber?" Pastor Eden asked, trying to shade his eyes from the rising sun.

"Yes, that's mentioned in The Book of Yasr." Freewheel added, "HUB destroyed it because it was designed for evil. HUB then confused the languages of the First People and scattered them all across the Seven Landmasses. This all occurred at the Tower of Jyber."

"I'm glad you've been reading, old friend!" Pastor Eden said, with a delighted grin. "We found it," he said, and his grin faded.

"No shit?" Freewheel said, fully understanding the consequences of finding such a place as the Tower of Jyber.

"That's where the phrase 'I can't understand their jibber jabber' comes from," the Pastor added knowingly. Pastor Eden knew he was reaching the discussion limit with his old teammate, so he followed up with his last question, expertly guiding Freewheel to discover his own conclusions.

He understood that Freewheel wasn't one for charity.

"Do you remember the 1st King that ruled the world and built the tower?"

"Yes, damnit!" Freewheel said, trying to keep from getting annoyed.

"Well, we have found his mummified body, and it's perfectly preserved."

Freewheel began to understand the weapon of mass destruction the Newtop Military was looking for. He still planned on turning in his resignation when he returned to Newtop, after he completed his final mission in Jyberjab. His last official report concluded that there were no weapons of destruction in all of Jyberjab. The Newtop Landmass Military ignored and shredded the report.

~

Before we started to jog outside to the Battle Rooms, Mr. Freewheel came to a halt and turned to the class, standing firmly. At the top of his lungs, as if speaking to an entire battalion, he ordered, "Pay attention today, or you'll pay with your asses in one way or another!" He paused for a moment, looked over the class, meeting every single student briefly in the eye.

"This shit could save your ass!"

Chapter 5

"We don't know the exact time a fruit will reveal itself, only HUB knows that, but by knowing what seeds to plant, you'll understand how to nourish your future. Seeds, like all living creatures, are known by their fruit."

-Parables of The Savior, the Old Book.

Mr. Eden was finishing up reading his favorite passage from the Old Book, displayed on an ancient brownstone alter, which stood before the entrance to a massive, secret library. Coincidentally, it had been his daughter's favorite quote as well. He smiled to himself as he walked away from the Old Book and entered the library. He had heard rumors of the library, which extended for a mile underneath the World Church, but of all the things he believed, he didn't believe it was a mile long.

To Mr. Eden's surprise, the rumors were true. The amount of books and information that filled the immense library astonished Mr. Eden. He happily accepted the paid internship at the secret library upon leaving the Newtop Military. He thought he could spend the rest of his life there and be completely happy. He was unaware that this idea wasn't too far from the truth. He would spend the rest of his life underneath the World Church. Just not in the library.

Within the first month of his internship at the World Church library, Mr. Eden found the information he was looking for...

~

"Many hundreds of years before the Great Drowning, the Sinpaz taught the most beautiful women of the New People how to read and write, the signs in the constellations and their meaning, how to create war and weapons of war, and, according to HUB, other useless knowledge. They fell in love with the women of the New People and created the giants of old. Many years after the Great Drowning, the Egybians of Egyb discovered the ancient texts and stone tablets containing the so-called useless knowledge. The information survived the Great

Drowning, and the discoverers used it to contact demons that roamed the post-flood New World. The discovers referred to themselves as the S.O.S., which stood for either Secret of Shadows to some, or Seller of Souls to others. They operated outside the laws of HUB and planned to resurrect their mummified leader. Their practices were forbidden.

The S.O.S. considered themselves enlightened and for hundreds of years they kept their knowledge hidden from the rest of the world. They operated in signs and symbols of antiquity in order to conceal their identity and confuse the world about their true intentions. Through occult practices, they were in contact with the Ventidos. Many high ranked S.O.S. members called upon the Ventidos by name. After all, their names were written in The Book of Enek."

Mr. Eden wrote down his findings on whatever paper he had available, usually writing his discoveries on old envelopes from letters he received from his family from clear across the world. He stuffed his notes within the pages of the two books that he was planning on mailing to his wife and daughter the next day. He knew that they would understand the significance of his findings and put the information to good use.

~

Mr. Eden was scheduled to meet the curator of the World Church the day he mailed the very important package to his family. The curator was rumored to be extremely intelligent and supposedly ran a small publishing company on the side. His name was Mr. Bookman. The things Mr. Bookman knew could fill a small library. Even if he burned them all down to the ground.

The little-known book publisher and curator, Mr. Bookman, knew each of the names of the Ventidos. He communicated with them daily. He loved and worshipped the leaders of the Sinpaz. Few knew that he was one of the leaders of the S.O.S. Even fewer people knew Mr. Bookman was possessed by one of their demons. Mr. Eden would be able to tell, from the pendant dangling from the curator's neck and from the signet ring that the curator wore, when they first met. Mr. Bookman's jewelry simply bore the numerals IIXX. Mr. Eden would know that it stood for Ventidos.

~

It was early in the evening at the World Church library. Mr. Eden was trying to finish gathering information about the untitled book he'd acquired in town earlier that day so he could jot down its brief description in the library's ledger.

"Mr. Eden, I presume," said the man, with a warm smile that looked like it was hiding bad intentions.

Mr. Eden looked up from his book. The light above his workspace came from a sky light that peeked into the library from above. Church members could look down at any time into the library, through the sky lights, as they walked across the red brick floor of the first level. At that time, Mr. Eden wasn't actually reading the book at all. He was simply staring at the wrinkled yellow pages while he daydreamed about his family. He missed his wife and his daughter very much. Mr. Eden hadn't seen them since he'd last brought home the ancient copy of the Old Book he had found at the underground library—the Old Book, which contained two new sections he'd never seen before. He really believed the purpose of their removal was to hide the origins of mankind from the human race, as a means to use the Old Book to control the world. He knew the World Church was planning world destruction. Now he knew who was running the World Church.

"I am Mr. Bookman," said the dark Egybian fellow. He was wearing a white suit and still awkwardly smiling as he extended his hand with the signet ring. "I am the curator of the World Church library. I've been out on holiday, and I am pleased to finally meet you."

Mr. Eden felt like he had recognized the curator from another time and place, but he couldn't quite place it. He took note of the black-beaded chain and pendant that dangled over Mr. Bookman's white suit. His mind wandered to thoughts of his recent military past and to the necklaces they wore that bore their name and rank. He also wondered, *Wasn't one of the members of Advanced Special Operations Unit Team 1, Egybian?*

Mr. Eden tried to hide the fact that he was anxious when he stood from his desk to shake hands with Mr. Bookman. He gained confidence in the fact that earlier that day he had sent his daughter the two sections that had been removed from the Old Book, along with an old legend he had come across in the ancient library. He took comfort knowing that the two sections he'd mailed his daughter were the only two copies of The Book of Enek and The Book of Yasr remaining in all of the Seven Landmasses. More importantly, he smiled inside knowing that they were fully stuffed with handwritten notes of the unknown society, the S.O.S. In his mind, Mr.

Eden was simply borrowing ancient books from the underground library, though he never planned to return them. He felt that he could help people by spreading the truth, which was often hidden in the past or locked away by wicked rulers in high places. His book rental was overdue, and Mr. Eden felt it. He knew that the curator would know exactly what books, and how many, were missing from the secret, underground World Church library.

"If you would please follow me," said Mr. Bookman, with an inviting smile only wolves were capable of making. "I would like to show you something you'll find very interesting."

~

Halfway around the world, the very same day, the orange-glowing sun slowly rose over the horizon at The College. Hilo woke in her bedroom loft when she heard the thud of something large hitting the floor and the pattering of many more thuds scurry across her living room below. She heard muffled whimpers coming from the room and decided to crawl to see who it was.

She peered over the ledge where the bamboo and bramble berry wood bookshelf stood. Down below, she saw three men in black masks scurrying around the fallen bookcase to sift through the hundreds of scattered books. Her mom was sitting on the futon, trying to fight back tears.

Clear plastic was draped all over the room. A makeshift curtain of more clear plastic divided the area where her mom was sitting from where the three masked men still searched through the scattered books. Hilo knew exactly what they were looking for. Weeks before, her mom received letters from Chiptech liaisons urging her to start selling Establishment medicines at Food Source Food Store. Naturally, she refused. Mrs. Eden's natural medicines and holistic healing practices worked. She understood the Establishment couldn't profit off of healthy people. Still, she would never sell the addictive, problematic, mass-produced, and unnatural prescription medicines from Chiptech, or any other mad scientist's lab, from any Establishment to make a living.

A man wearing a black mask and yellow-striped fedora was sitting next to Hilo's mom holding a gun to her head. There was a contraption attached to her mom's right arm that connected all the way up to her shoulder. It looked like a sturdy black cast or some kind of shoulder pad with a gauntlet attached to the end, held together by a web of wire. At the very end of the contraption, in the hand of Mrs. Eden, was a stainless steel pistol, pointed under her chin. What could only be described as a puppet string was being held by the black-masked man in the yellow-striped fedora. For the third time he asked Mrs. Eden where the information was. She shook her head no again, fully understanding the consequences. Mrs. Eden shut her eyes, blinking away tears.

Hilo heard a loud bang. She used both hands to conceal her yelp. The men didn't find anything, but they took away everything.

~

Mr. Eden was standing next to Mr. Bookman on an ancient stone bridge that led to a chamber located even further beneath the World Church. The chamber was older than the Stone Triangle Temples and was lit by flaming red torches. It was eerily cold, even standing above the lava flow that circled around the moat surrounding the chamber. In the center, there were computers translating the many different incantations that hooded church members were chanting in unison. The church members looked faceless and were covered in royal blue robes. Mr. Eden wondered whether they were floating. From the first looks of it, Mr. Eden already knew that he did not want to be down there.

Their spells were translated into a single language that Mr. Eden was somewhat familiar with. Throughout his research, Mr. Eden had come across similar sounding words, and finally concluded that the computers the robed men were chanting into were translating the different incantations into one, single language. It was a language that first existed following the Great Drowning. The language of the New People. The language spoken by the 1st King. The anti-savior written in the Old Book that would deceive the entire world, Apleon.

In the far ends of the round room, rituals of all kinds were performed as the voices of the robed church members grew louder. Mr. Eden wished he hadn't seen the kinds of unholy rituals that were taking place in front of him. Chills went up his spine when he noticed the object in the center of the room that laid upon a stone altar. He knew that it had come from the bottomless pit because he had been there when it was pulled up. The object was being bombarded with the sound of a slow, ancient chant from speakers who ominously hung from the ceiling, pointing directly at it. Mr. Eden couldn't understand all of the words that reverberated throughout the chamber. Dark spirits danced in sinuous circles around the object.

The chanting stopped when the object in the center of the room burst to life and jumped from the stone altar. Mr. Eden's eyes widened, and he felt that he couldn't move when the mummified body of the 1st King rushed towards him.

~

"Our Task Unit Commander sends his regards," Mr. Bookman said, as he left the chamber smiling like he had destroyed the sun.

Chapter 6

Time couldn't have moved any slower, I thought. I was planning on heading to Computer City to meet up with Justin and Anne-Marie, but not before I got breakfast—a fresh cup of Rocky's coffee. I anxiously stood inside of Rocky's Coffee shop, studying the warm colors of the yellow sunrise, while waiting for fresh coffee to finish brewing. Yesterday, Justin told me that he had the codes to access the encrypted Shadow Pages of the Network.

~

As usual, I could tell that Ms. Snicth wasn't excited to see me waiting at the doors of the campus library before they opened. I was shot down verbally each time I tried to be courteous with Ms. Snicth that morning. I figured it didn't matter. I actually enjoyed the rejection and indulged in Ms. Snicth's irritation. She was fun to talk to, I thought, especially really early in the morning.

"Why do you want to bother me so early, Henry? Why can't you just be like the rest of the college students and sleep?"

"'Cause I figure one of these days, Ms. Snicth, you'll have a smile on your face the minute you lay eyes on me," I said. "Besides, I really do like your accent. It's beautiful."

She glared, although I was being honest. I thought to myself that one day I ought to test her personality out in the evening. Maybe then I could see her smile for once when I was around.

~

Justin and Anne-Marie walked into the library unnoticed by Ms. Snicth. I was a glutton for new information, and Justin could tell how excited I was to finally see beyond the Shadow Pages. I couldn't wait to get my hands on the access codes to see what was hiding on the back pages of the Network. In the back of my mind, I couldn't help but wonder how he had gotten ahold of the access codes to the Shadow Pages in the first place. Besides Ms. Snicth, we were the only three people in the library.

~

Though I felt that it was probably in our best interests to keep what we saw on the Shadow Pages to ourselves, Justin encouraged me to include everything that I had learned that day into my history thesis. After all, I thought, that's what friends are for.

Justin helped me see the way everything was all connected—from the Old Book to the Shadow Pages—in a great attempt to erase any mention of The Savior from the history books and, eventually, the entire world. Everything from poisoning our land, air, food, and water to erasing entire histories of ancient civilizations was meant to hide the fact that the Establishment leaders, from all of the Seven Landmasses, were planning on placing their own savior in charge—the great deceiver who would sit on the throne of The Great Temple that was currently being rebuilt for the third and final time.

All I kept thinking was that the information we found that day would end up getting us all killed. Eventually, I finished writing for the morning and was grateful for Justin's guidance, even if I ended up ruffling a few feathers. Money didn't come easy.

~

I bent over to get my computer card out of my pack to save my progress when Ms. Snicth hollered, "What the hell are you doing, Henry?"

Mr. Beandrop looked up from a nearby computer at me. I looked at him and at Ms. Snicth when I finally realized I'd forgotten to close out of the last site I was browsing on the Shadow Pages. I thought, *When did he arrive?* The thought vanished when I suddenly noticed every monitor in Computer City going haywire. White lights from the monitors were rapidly flashing on and off like a message was being sent in Morse Code. I could hear robots speaking gibberish traveling through the wires that connected every computer to the main power source below the library. The alarm stopped when I finally closed out of the Shadow page. The page was titled, "New Landmass Order."

Justin and Anne-Marie were nowhere to be found. I wasn't allowed back at Computer City. Ms. Snicth banned me that morning.

~

I was deflated because I couldn't return to the library to finish typing the rest of my thesis. I worried about how I could ever make money from a half-finished work that was supposed to live up to the standards of the Old Book. To top it off, I was overwhelmed with the flood of information from the secret Network Shadow Pages and completely burned out with schoolwork. As I left the library that morning, I decided to turn in what I had written so far to Mr. Beandrop. At any rate, Mr. Beandrop wanted to meet with each of his students to discuss their progress before Midterm Break. I figured today was the best day to meet with him. I didn't care to finish my thesis or even pass History IV class anymore. I knew I wasn't going to graduate.

I handed in my half-written thesis to Mr. Beandrop and was instructed to return to his office in the History Department Building when he finished his class lectures later on that evening. I tried to see the positive side that morning and decided that even if I came up short, I knew I had done my best. That's all that mattered. It was better to have finished working on my thesis before I went to visit my family in San Thiago during the week of Midterm Break anyway.

~

Chess moves that were planned out thousands of years ago were in movement that day.

A Cruise Vessel stopped at the coldest Island Landmass to explore Nutrisource. In the weeks to follow, the same ship would stop at different ports for the passengers to vacation all around the Seven Landmasses. The people inside were carrying a virus and didn't know it. The virus was easily transmitted once in the air and genetically engineered at the Source. The passengers acquired the virus through apples engineered by Robert Fencewood at Nutrisource.

The virus would stimulate the entire lockdown of the world. Every and all businesses would shut down, and people would not be allowed out in public. Strict distancing laws would be set in place, and the people around the entire world would be forced to cover their faces with masks to stop the spread. Everyone would go crazy and start sanitizing everything, not knowing that they were building a super virus. Even worse, they helped implement the cashless society.

Everyone would prefer to use computers and shop virtually on the Network to avoid going out in public. Cash handling would be deemed dangerous, and all people, both small and great, rich and poor, free and bound, would eventually need to get chipped to process all financial transactions. The mark of the Anti-Savior would be tied to the chip and the global economy. Those who refused the mark were automatically cut off from the global economy. The chip would be required for all buying and selling.

~

Billionaire Robert Fencewood and Mr. Bookman waited to board a Whitechopper along with a new guest. He had gone by many names in times past and planned on replacing HUB when he took a seat in The Great Temple, but that day he was known only as Rey. He was dressed in a blood red suit.

Fencewood, Bookman, and Rey understood all of this. They boarded the Whitechopper as soon as the Cruise Vessel embarked towards the Island Landmass, where The College was. They would arrive at The College before the Cruise Vessel. They carried with them new Chiptech technology that would revolutionize the way money was used in the world. The College would be ground zero for great suffering around the entire world.

The Central Intelligence Office of Newtop Landmass received an encrypted message that day. It originated from the library at The College.

The message read: *New Landmass Order*. The entire Newtop Military prepared for deployment to bases all around the Landmasses.

~

"You wanted to see me?" I asked, as I entered Mr. Beandrop's office. It was cozy, though it was absolutely filled with books in every corner. There wasn't any room for chairs amongst his book collection. I wasn't surprised to see Mr. Beandrop sitting on a stack of books from behind his small, lamplit desk, reading over my thesis.

Mr. Beandrop had a large window behind his desk that let in a breathtaking view of the ocean and cascading tropical jungle outside. The jungle connected to a beach that was caressed gently by the warm, glowing sunset and blueish-pink and orange ocean waves.

"Ahhh, Mr. Gomez, how do you do? Please come in and take a seat on a stack!" Mr. Beandrop said with pride and joy. He pointed around the room, gesturing towards the many stacks of books that lined his office walls.

It smelled like vanilla and roasted coffee inside of the cozy archive that was Mr. Beandrop's office—the coffee smell most likely coming from the half-empty white mug on his desk. I could tell that Mr. Beandrop had already forgotten about the recent events of my fiasco at Computer City. Besides being jolly, Mr. Beandrop was very affable. I let that observation calm me as I took a seat on a small book stack nearest the large window.

"I have read your thesis and, although it's a little short, I still think that you have made some interesting points, Henry," he said, as he licked his finger to help turn a few more pages. "Without a doubt, I will be cross-checking your many works cited to determine if what you've come up with is accurate. However, I am most curious to know about where you obtained this kind of information. In all of my years as College faculty, I have never heard of anything like this before," he said, sounding like I had shaken him to his jolly core.

I couldn't tell by his tone whether that was a good thing or a bad thing. I sat silently knowing that it was better to let Mr. Beandrop do most of the talking for the rest of my progress report. The last thing I wanted to do was open my mouth and possibly end up saying something out of haste that would cause me more trouble that day. Being banned from the library was more than enough for me to deal with. I waited on the stack of books, observing the soft setting sun, until Mr. Beandrop spoke.

"I would like to share your thesis with some friends of mine who would find this kind of information very valuable," Mr. Beandrop said, then looked up from reading my thesis to meet my eye. "If there is any merit to your information, you could possibly stand to make a lot of money!" He threw his hands up like he had played a trick on the world, then returned to his jovial state. All of the tensions inside of me subsided.

"What kind of friends are we talking about?" I asked, looking like I was trying to read Mr. Beandrop's mind.

"The kind of friends who can help get your information out properly, my boy!" Mr. Beandrop specified joyfully. He paused for effect, leaned over in my direction, and said cheerfully, "A small book publisher and a billionaire of course!"

~

I was exhausted from the many events of the day, but my brief evening shift scrubbing pots and pans in the back kitchen sink of FSFS was more than enough to lift my spirits. I found comfort in the small tasks that took my mind off of the overwhelming burdens that often followed increased knowledge. Moreover, Hilo invited me over to have tea and discuss what I had discovered within the Shadow Pages of the Network—only after I finished washing the dishes. No matter how exhausted I was, I couldn't pass up the offer to spend time with Hilo. More importantly, I desperately wanted to talk to someone else who wouldn't judge me for expressing myself. What I had learned from the Shadow Pages depressed me. For some reason, I knew that Hilo would understand.

~

Hilo gave me a knowing look as she got up to fix herself another cup of tea in the kitchen, like she was bored that everything I had told her that night was old news. I was working on my eleventh beer to help me forget the long day.

"Not all of us have a library like yours, Hilo," I said, loud enough so she could hear me from the kitchen. "I've never heard about the Census Killings before the Shadow Pages. It was never mentioned in any of the history books," I said honestly and more open than I had ever been around Hilo.

"I'm just worried about how you were able to even access the Shadow Pages, Henry," Hilo said from the kitchen. Under the influence of seven beers, I eventually told her about my friend Justin for the first time earlier that night. She was right about being worried for accessing the Shadow Pages, but I knew deep down that Justin was no harm. I was more worried about the way the computers had gone berserk that morning.

"You could've transmitted a message to people you really don't want to mess with, Henry," Hilo warned. Flashing computer monitors blinked in my head when Hilo confirmed my worries. I ignored her statement and drank more of my beer, waiting for her to return from the kitchen. I brushed the uncomfortable thought off and decided to steer the topic back to the Census Killings.

"I can't believe they supported strict gun control laws and basically gave up their weapons," I continued telling Hilo—trying to hopefully get over the event that had happened about a century ago. "It made it easier for the foreign military police to lead them to the slaughter," I said, then took a huge swig of beer.

Learning about alien technologies that the militaries already had in their possession, which nobody else would know about for years, or Establishments of every Landmass poisoning the soil, air, food, and water as a means of decreasing the population, or the Burning of Books to cover up ancient knowledge was a lot easier for me to take in at that moment. "If I ever go down at the hands of a wicked Establishment leader," I said, realizing I was starting to feel a little buzzed, "I will at least go down standing up. Guns blazing."

It was silent for a while. Hilo returned with a hot cup of tea and another cold beer. The last of my 12-pack of beers. I seized the opportunity to flirt with her while I was still coherent. With a cunning smile, I confidently asked, "Are you trying to get me drunk to get more information out of me, or are you planning on seducing me tonight, Ms. Hilo Eden?"

Hilo didn't respond. She just stared at me, smiling warmly, standing with our drinks at the foot of the futon. We held eyes for a long moment of silence. I felt like she could see what I was thinking. I felt like everything was falling into place at that moment. At the time, I didn't know that whenever a woman is comfortable around a man, that every and any time is the perfect time to kiss her. The moment had passed. I didn't make a move and missed an opportunity to finally kiss Hilo. In my mind, I felt like I had missed the greatest opportunity of my life. Hilo expertly changed the subject.

She smiled and handed me the ice-cold beer, then took a seat closer to me on the oat-colored futon and said, "It's called history because he who wins the war gets to write the story."

I tried to think about what she'd just said before she playfully nudged me and added, "Get it? His Story."

I smiled, finally understanding what she meant. She took a sip of tea, then rested her head on my shoulder. This was the closest I had ever been to Hilo, and I treated the moment with the highest respect. I felt like I was carrying the last drop of water across a thousand miles of uncharted desert. I learned a lot that day, and the lessons kept coming to me. I kept my mouth shut and finally learned why gentlemen rarely say much. I finally understood that speaking would only ruin moments like this. The warmth of her body next to mine helped me forget about all of the day's problems better than any beer could do. It also helped ease away any regrets I had lingering inside of me for having missed the perfect opportunity to finally kiss her. I finished my eleventh beer and began sipping the fresh, cold one Hilo had just given me. Beer tasted better coming from her. We sat together for a while before she broke the silence and shattered any more hopes I had of kissing her that night.

"It shouldn't be surprising that an Establishment leader would use information provided in confidence on a census form to kill millions of people," Hilo said. We were back to business. She continued, saying, "Besides killing off an entire race, wars are often created for personal gain to control natural resources and enslave people in one way or another. I think the real question that's bothering you, Henry, from all that you've uncovered today is, 'Why would the Establishment hide information about the census killings within the Shadow Pages and remove an important part of human history from the classroom?'"

Her point hit home. I quietly thought for a while. It didn't take long for me to realize, as I said out loud, "Because they're planning on doing it again."

Hilo's guidance in helping me understand the bigger picture amazed me. She reminded me of Justin the way that she expertly guided me to discover my own answers. My amazement was short-lived when I realized that I had just learned another depressing lesson for the day—the plan was to kill everyone that believed in The Savior.

"Exactly!" she exclaimed, and I was stunned by her excitement. "Now here is the real brain teaser. *Who* is behind the Shadow Pages?" she asked, nearly jumping from the futon.

We sat next to each other in another comfortable silence for the second time that night, while I tried to figure out who was behind the Shadow Pages or whether I should kiss her or not. Who could be the ones still connected to the fallen Innumerable Lights of old? The ones who were trying to erase all knowledge of the truth and create their own New World? The ones trying to be like HUB? I drank the last of my beer before I finally answered Hilo's question.

"The people planning the next mass killing," I said sarcastically, fishing for clues because I was tired of thinking, drowsy, and actually starting to feel the full effects of all of the beer I had drunk that night.

"Think, Henry," she demanded, with a look that said I feel like slapping you for finishing all of that damn beer. Although I was obviously drunk and tired, she intrigued me even more with her patience for me in my drunken state. I thought it stemmed from having to help people during her Exercise Therapy Lessons. They were the kind of people who needed help and extra coaching to finally see that everything came from within. Hilo was patient and strong. And at that drunken moment, all I could think about was how beautiful she was. The only other thought that ran through my head was that I was tired of thinking about the destruction of the world. I could tell that Hilo wanted to talk more. She was very passionate, especially about "Saving and helping others," as she put it.

All I wanted to do was just listen to the sound of her voice and be next to her for the rest of that night. But since she was my boss, and I didn't want to lose her respect, I tried hard to focus on our conversation.

Hilo repeated herself a little more seriously. "Who do you think is behind the Shadow Pages?"

Intoxicated, I thought back, with great effort, to my half-finished thesis. I tried to think past the many beers that were affecting my train of thought. I remembered what I had written and submitted to Mr. Beandrop. In all of my research, I had concluded that everything was connected in an effort to hide The Savior from the New World so nobody could ever access the First World again. But Hilo already knew that. After all, I thought, Hilo was the one who had loaned me the books that led to that conclusion. She obviously knew about the Sinpaz and their twenty-two leaders, the Ventidos. Hilo already knew more about the information that filled my thesis long before I ever did.

After much thought, I really didn't know the answer to her question and simply said, "I don't know."

"I'll give you a hint: it's the same people you unintentionally contacted at Computer City this morning, possibly starting another world war," she said jokingly and hit me hard on my left shoulder. My eyes were feeling heavy, and the empty beer bottle in my hand felt like it was weightless. I closed my eyes for a bit.

Before I passed out completely on Hilo's oat-colored futon, I remembered thinking that Hilo didn't drink alcohol. It made her even more attractive to me. I fell in love with Hilo that night and struggled to listen to anything more that she had to say.

Hilo followed her own question with another, not realizing that I was half-asleep and completely drunk when she asked, "You ever heard of the Sellers of Souls, Henry?"

I was dosing off and don't ever remember asking, "The who?"

I fell asleep thinking, *Why is alcohol legal but holistic medicine from natural sources considered illegal?* I was too drunk and tired to focus on Hilo. I fell asleep while trying to answer my own question.

Chapter 7

"You're fired," Hilo said with a smile, then she handed me a fresh cup of coffee as I lay disoriented, wrapped in a tea-green sheet, on the oat-colored futon. I held the coffee out in front of me trying to blink away the constant rhythm pounding inside of my aching head.

"You were really drunk last night," Hilo said, looking me over. She was holding her own fresh cup of steaming coffee in hand.

"Who is behind the Shadow Pages?" I finally asked. The fact that I was coherent enough to recall most of our conversation from the night before surprised Hilo.

"I'll tell you after breakfast," Hilo said and turned to walk into her dimly-lit kitchen. I noticed she was wearing plaid boxer shorts and a white tank top. The sun hadn't come up yet. I thought it must have also been hungover that early, cloudy morning.

~

A Whitechopper landed on the campus front lawn of The College. Mr. Beandrop excitedly stumbled across the green campus lawn as he ran to greet the men who were filing out of the Whitechopper door labeled, Chiptech CEO.

"Hello there! I'm so delighted to see you guys!" Mr. Beandrop said, eager to greet the important guests. Mr. Beandrop struggled to suppress his delight and maintain his professionalism.

Billionaire Robert Fencewood's yellow-striped fedora blew off from the spinning blades of the Whitechopper, and he retrieved it, dusting grass off its brim. Dust and blades of grass were blowing around the campus lawn. Students heading to class strolled by, only minding their pocket phones like there wasn't a care in the world.

"Thank you for reaching out to us, Beandrop. The information you've shared with us is most interesting," said the man dressed in all white wearing a grin only seen amongst evil clowns. He continued. "Mr. Fencewood and I both agreed to come as soon as we could."

Before going to have lunch that afternoon, they headed to the History Department Building to grab Henry's History IV thesis, which was resting on a stack of books in Mr. Beandrop's office.

"I am looking forward to meeting the boy who wrote it," said Mr. Bookman, as a long, sinister grin stretched across his face. Mr. Beandrop smiled cheerfully, clasping his pudgy hands together out in front of him. This was the greatest moment of Mr. Beandrop's happy life.

A third man slowly stepped out from the White-chopper whom Mr. Beandrop had never met before. He looked charming. He resembled a prince from *Old Hendrix's Bedtime Stories* and was also suited—but in all red. Mr. Bookman and Robert Fencewood didn't bother to introduce the third man. Mr. Beandrop was too excited and didn't bother to ask who he was anyway. Rey followed the men around like a king observing the many moves of his army on the battlefield.

~

"My dad sent me handwritten notes that described the S.O.S. and their involvement with ancient prophecy, in great detail," Hilo explained, as we rode down an old-fashioned freight elevator, deep under FSFS. The whole time I'd worked there, I'd never noticed what was right beneath my feet. I found it hard to concentrate on what Hilo was telling me.

"Every Shadow Page, secret plan, world war, and catastrophe you can think of can be traced back to the Sellers of Souls. I call them Sacks of Shit," Hilo said, and it took me off guard hearing her curse. "These bastards think they're special and only invite people into their secret organization who they believe can keep a secret. They refer to themselves as the Secret of Shadows. Personally, I think they only keep pawns they can easily brainwash and dispose of to use for their hidden organization's plans to dominate the entire world."

When we reached the bottom level, I lifted the wooden freight elevator door and followed Hilo into an expanse that was glowing like the sun. An entire ecosystem existed beneath FSFS. No wonder where Hilo got all of the fresh food and ingredients she sold at her store.

"This is my farm," she said proudly, as we entered the bright room. I stood in the Garden of the First World. Plants and fruits of all kinds were growing under hundreds of lights and inside plastic tubing, resting happily above running water and what looked like some kind of lazy, turquoise-colored grass. I heard the sound of a waterfall falling in the distance, and it felt like we were in the rainforest. In one corner of the farm, there were giant sprinklers suspended by hoses gently watering crops of all kinds. In another area, there were little sprouts in small, humid plastic domes under many gentle glowing white lights hanging from ropes. White puffy clouds slowly drifted above. A half-rainbow drooped from the ceiling. It smelled like herbs and wet wood, like a field of flowers and the smell of rainfall in the tropics. So many fragrances touched my senses as we walked around Hilo's many gardens.

There were vegetables of all kinds and even marijuana was growing in another section of the farm. There were barrels and bags labeled with many different names of plants, seeds, and fertilizers. There was a large fish hatchery and even a chicken coup. There was a pasture where donkeys, goats, pigs, and a few cows grazed beneath FSFS. A small red barn housed other things I could not see. The best part was the freshwater pond surrounded by all kinds of fruit trees—mangos, avocados, oranges, lemons and limes, as well as other fruits I was unfamiliar with. A few boxes of beehives with honey bees, swarming in and out, surrounded the far left corner of the garden.

Before I could ask how she was able to build everything beneath FSFS, Hilo started talking. "My mom was one of the last Native Healers from Newtop Landmass who believed that the land, air, and water were sacred. My mom always said, 'You cannot eat money when everything else is gone.'"

For the first time, I noticed bees pollinating the many flowers. Ducks nibbling on some kind of grain quacked as we walked by.

"Seeds were valued as precious information because they provided the sustenance for the survival of her people—a people who were forced onto Newtop Landmass Reservations where their traditions were destroyed, along with their knowledge. My people," Hilo said, as she stopped to look at me. "They used a barter system, trading both actual seeds and what was referred to as 'knowledge seeds,' as currency," Hilo explained, as I took in everything around me.

I walked next to Hilo in silence for quite some time along the many garden rows and many lines of fruit trees next to the pond before she spoke again. "I guess this is my inheritance. Knowledge on how to provide for myself. Not many people know how to grow crops anymore, let alone know how to live independent of any Establishment. On top of that, not many people care to research and learn how to do for themselves anymore. Even with our many advancements in technology. It scares me, Henry," Hilo said, as we walked down one of the many garden aisles lined with raspberry and blackberry bushes. We walked on a small stone bridge over a small river that peacefully meandered throughout the garden and around the lines of bushes.

"What scares me the most is the fact that there are no seeds left to sustain ourselves, even if we wanted to start a garden like yours, Hilo," I said, remembering the many seedless foods sold in stores supplied by the Establishment.

Hilo and I walked a short while in silence before she considered my point and then began saying, "I grow everything here because I know it is not altered by Establishment scientists. My parents taught me that seeds of all kinds are sacred and should be left alone. The most precious seeds being the seeds of life and the seeds that grow food. Food is our medicine," Hilo explained. "My parents were killed for trying to help people live a long and healthy life—mentally, physically, and spiritually—and pass along their knowledge and their seeds. They understood that the Establishment couldn't profit off healthy people."

"I understand," I said, taking Hilo's hand in mine. There was nothing more I could say. Besides, I had just learned more about Hilo and what really happened to her parents.

We walked silently around the vast garden of Hilo Eden. Thoughts were circling in my head when I remembered a flyer on campus that paid students to submit their grocery receipts to some sketchy Network site. It dawned on me that they were studying our buying trends to know where to target. I kept my mouth shut and tried to enjoy the many experiences of being surrounded by unaltered creation, firsthand. Most of all, I wanted to enjoy being next to Hilo. Maybe an opportunity to kiss her would present itself.

We turned around a corner of apple trees, red and green apples hanging from the branches, and I was surprised to run into Professor U. He was raking the leaves around the many trees in the garden wearing Far East slippers, overalls, a white T-shirt, and a Far Eastern hat on top of his head.

"It is better to be a warrior in a garden, than a gardener in a war," said Professor U. without looking up from the leaves he was raking as we approached him from the rear.

"Professor, what are you doing here?" I asked, surprised.

"Professor U. was a gardener back in his country," Hilo said. "He has made many improvements in my farm and in exchange for him being able to 'relax his mind,' as he puts it, I get to have one private lesson a week in Jiu-Jitsu with him," said Hilo proudly.

"No wonder where you learned all of those moves you submitted me with in training!" I said, smiling. I felt like I had been taking advantage of, and I promised I would give Hilo a run for the money at class that night.

"Be seeing you," Professor U. said, and then he started to laugh as we walked away.

~

That night at Jiu-Jitsu class, Hilo struggled to submit me. I gave her a good run, but her private lessons with Professor U. paid off when, about three minutes into our roll, she ended up heel-hooking me. Inside I was frustrated, and I could tell her head grew a little bigger. She was barely a purple belt, and I had just received my black belt. Upon tapping out to her submission, I noticed Professor U. smiling in approval. Out of the corner of my eye, I caught a glimpse of someone peering through the academy front window. It was a man dressed in all white, smiling like a wolf who had just spotted an easy dinner. The power flickered on and off a few times mid-training, and there wasn't a sound coming from the normally noisy night, full of croaking frogs and chirping crickets, outside of the academy.

Professor U. looked in that direction, then back at me, and laughed his contagious laugh. I laughed, too, in spite of myself, and Hilo started laughing. I was confused as to what we were laughing about, then Professor U. broke the silence. "Good job, Hilo!" We all laughed again. I looked back outside of the Jiu-Jitsu academy, and the man in the white suit was gone.

$\sim$

Mr. Beandrop wanted to meet with me to discuss my thesis with his friends the next day. Since Hilo could help explain the contents of my thesis in better detail, I invited her along. Hilo and I waited at a table in the bustling Tivoli Tavern for the guests to arrive. Mr. Beandrop had arrived early and was excited, as usual. He got up to order a couple of pitchers of beer and one sparkling water for Hilo.

I saw Justin and Anne-Marie talking to two suited men outside of the Tivoli Tavern. They looked like they were talking about something of great importance; however, the two suited men looked more tense than Justin. Like they were being scolded. I felt like I could see their discomfort flee from their bodies as the two suited men were left standing in their tracks. Like Justin had just ripped them a new one for not following orders. No one looked happy afterward, and the only one who forced an awful smile was the one in all white.

A thought ran through my head that this would be the perfect time to introduce Hilo to Justin and Anne-Marie. I hopped up out of my seat in the tavern to go and get the couple. I had no idea at the time that the two suited men were Mr. Beandrop's friends.

Mr. Beandrop interrupted my pursuit. "What kind of appetizers should we get?" He bumped into me as I tried to leave the noisy college tavern. The power cut off, then quickly regenerated.

I ignored him and the power outage so I could catch up to Justin and Anne-Marie. They were rounding the Tivoli Tavern corner. By the time I got outside, Justin and Anne-Marie were nowhere to be found.

After a few minutes of awkwardly standing outside wondering where the couple had gone, I decided to head back into the busy campus tavern. I followed the two suited men into the tavern and overheard a little of their conversation as they removed their sports coats and one removed his yellow-striped fedora, hanging it on a coat rack that lined the brick entrance wall to the bustling college bar.

"......The time is at hand. We need to move quicker to implement the changes for our plan to be successful throughout the world," said the man in all white. "Nothing must be left to chance," Mr. Bookman said, as he approached the table where Mr. Beandrop and Hilo sat.

Hilo didn't notice Robert Fencewood remove his yellow-striped fedora and hang it next to his sports coat on the coat rack before he entered the tavern. I arrived at our table, shortly before the suited guests, and overheard Mr. Beandrop discussing the details of my thesis with Hilo. She was a better communicator and more knowledgeable about my thesis, and by the way she looked that day, anyone with a good head on their shoulders could not help but pay attention to her. She was wearing a white blouse and black skirt. She wore a red ribbon in her hair and looked stunning. I felt lucky to be with her that special day.

"What I'm trying to understand, Ms. Eden, is how do you communicate the name of the one Savior, as you say, to so many people around the world when there are so many different languages?" Mr. Beandrop asked.

"Ask anyone around the world who the 'Way' and who the 'Light' of the world is, and I'm willing to bet that nine out of ten people will mention The Savior's name, even if they follow another agreement," Hilo said. "The Savior's name is immediately recognizable to alleviate confusion around the world."

"Well, how do we know that when we use the many names for the Anti-Savior that we are speaking about the same person?" Mr. Beandrop asked.

"All men knew HUB before and after the Great Drowning, even the 1st King that turned evil when he started to worship his own idols in place of HUB. The Anti-Savior has many names due to the fact that he was present at the Tower of Jyber when HUB confounded the languages of the New

People and scattered them across the Seven Land-masses," Hilo said. "Everyone around the world is talking about the 1st King even if they are using different names to describe him." Hilo opened up her copy of The Old Book, along with The Book of Enek and The Book of Yasr to prove her point to Mr. Beandrop.

The two suited men approached as Hilo finished talking. "Your books look very interesting," Mr. Bookman said, as he approached the table, interrupting Hilo and Mr. Beandrop's conversation. The Tavern lights flickered, and Hilo grabbed my hand. I couldn't tell whether she was excited for my book publishing deal or scared.

"Ah, jolly good, our guests have arrived! Without further adieu, Mr. Bookman and Robert Fencewood, I would like you to meet Henry Gomez and Hilo Eden!" Mr. Beandrop said, obviously overjoyed.

"I am honored to put a face to a name," Mr. Bookman said, as he extended his signet-ringed hand to shake mine. Hilo's eyes widened as she caught a glimpse of the ring he wore. She stood up suddenly, as if she had sat on a needle.

"We have to go," Hilo said, looking me in the eye.

I didn't trust her judgment. I didn't recognize that the man in all white was the same man who had stared in the window of the Jiu-Jitsu academy the previous night. I didn't see that she was frightened and was looking to me for support. I was young and naive in the ways of women.

"This is my chance to make some real money," I said to Hilo. The words came out of nowhere, and I did not mean for them to come out disrespectful. Hilo looked at me like I was crazy. After all, I had learned so much from her and so much about her. I tried to justify myself and only made things worse, when in front of the new guests I said, "Not all of us own a business, Hilo. This is my opportunity."

Hilo looked at me in disbelief, then she gracefully left the Tivoli Tavern with her books. Although Mr. Beandrop had spilled the beans without knowing it, I knew that I had ruined everything that day.

~

Rey paid a visit to FSFS while Hilo was with me at the Tivoli Tavern. He placed a single, virus-infected red apple on top of the organic red apples at FSFS. Food Source Food Store became ground zero for the pandemic of 2020.

Chapter 8

They were silent as a whisper, but their presence hushed the surrounding landscape. Hundreds of troops rushed the beaches as the moon smiled upon the sands and kissed the surrounding ocean. An invisible barrier was set in place around all ends of the island where The College was located. No one in. No one out.

~

Henzo Yookimura led Advanced Special Operations Unit Team 1 to the crash site. The Newtop military named the site Area 1551.

"Approaching the site, sir," said Henzo, communicating with headquarters via radio. "The rest of the unit, secure the perimeter. Fencewood and Bookman, follow me."

"Yes, sir!" the two said in unison, as the three slowly approached the crash site. Smoke was everywhere, and there were pieces of twisted metal amongst small burning fires. In the center of the site, there was a hole and the remaining half of the ship that had crashed. It was grey in color, and none of the soldiers of Team 1 had ever seen anything like it before.

They approached the crashed object cautiously when they heard a door slide open. On the door there were engravings that looked like numerals, and all that was legible was what looked like two slashes and an X on the left side of the door. Inside, there were three beings still buckled into seats. They were unconscious but still alive. They were not the size of a normal person, and they were grey in color, with eyes that looked like thick, black circles.

Before Task Unit 1 Commander Henzo Yookimura and his wingmen approached farther inside to check on the barely conscious beings, he received a radio transmission. "Stand down, Yookimura. Do not approach. I repeat, do not approach."

"Yes, sir," Henzo said.

"You are to report back to your Warchopper. Your assistance is needed in the Arctic Ring of Frozen Waters. Your coordinates and details await. Over and out."

"Let's move out!" Henzo ordered.

As they left the crash site, Henzo witnessed a team dressed in special white suites approaching the site. He figured it was best that they left the site uncontaminated.

The technology inside of the crashed ship wasn't like anything Team 1 had ever seen before. This predated computers by nearly 34 years. Nothing in any of the Seven Landmasses was the same afterwards. The military blamed the crash landing on weather technology. The three surviving beings at Area 1551 were kept top secret. They were able to return to their home beneath the ocean after Newtop Military interrogation.

~

The Task Unit 2 Commander walked down a grey corridor at a Newtop Military Base stationed at the Arctic Ring of Frozen Waters. She was surprised it was a warm 72 degrees despite it being below freezing outside. Her team, Advanced Special Operations Unit Team 2, had just finished unloading the massive cargo they had brought back from deep within the Frozen Waters. She headed to the Chief Newtop Military Commander's office to debrief before her unit finished unloading the red-headed giant and the rest of the remains of Team 1. Down one hallway in the snow-covered base, she noticed three men in isolation. They were the three only surviving members of Advanced Special Operations Unit Team 1. Her curiosity got the best of her, and she stood behind a plastic and glass barrier, staring into the room. She read the names on the front of their hospital beds: Fencewood, R.; Bookman, A.; and Yookimura, H.

She was staring at the men lying hooked up to respirators. She noticed they would twitch every now and then and acted as if they were trying to force something out of their bodies. They were possessed by demons, and she didn't have a clue that they were being taken over as she observed. Their faces were distorted, making them hard for the Commander to ever recognize who they were. All she had to go on was their names.

Freewheel and Pastor Eden came walking down the hallway.

"I would've rather been eaten by that giant we killed than be like one of the men in that room," Pastor Eden said to Freewheel and to his Task Unit Commander.

"You ain't got any spirit binding prayers or spells to cast out their demons?" Freewheel asked.

"It isn't a spell or prayer. It's faith that overcomes that type of danger," Pastor Eden said to the two of them still staring into the glass windows. The men inside thrashed violently trying to rid themselves of the straps that held them down like rabid animals.

"We're gonna need some faith and a shit-ton of firepower," said Freewheel. The three sat staring at the wild men. The air was colder and the corridor was flashing like a strobe light. Before heading to debrief with the Chief Commander from the "Giant Operation," as the team referred to it, the three stood and stared. It was all they could do.

"What do you think, Commander?" Freewheel asked the Commander of Team 2.

"I think we'll need some firepower and a shit-ton of faith," said Task Unit 2 Commander Snicth.

~

Mr. Freewheel and Ms. Snicth looked on as soldiers from Newtop Landmass stormed the beach that night. The soldiers set up roadblocks along the roads that surrounded the Island Landmass The College was on. There were soldiers unloading ammunition and crates onto the beaches. There were tents along the beach of the island.

Ms. Snicth and Mr. Freewheel looked at each other deciding what would be their best plan of action. They could easily blow up the small army that landed on the island, but killing innocent people for no reason was not their style.

"It's started," said Ms. Snicth. "Go and gather the rebels. We need to move off this Island and secure a safer operating position."

"Yes, Commander," said Mr. Freewheel.

Mr. Freewheel's first thought was to get Hilo Eden. He was already dressed in Newtop fatigues and carrying enough ammunition and guns on his person.

The two ran in separate directions to prepare for their escape. They were gonna need a lot of trained soldiers and firepower. Luckily, Mr. Freewheel knew where to gather more men.

~

Mr. Freewheel was at Hilo's apartment loft above FSFS. He handed her instructions, along with a fully loaded assault rifle, a handgun, and seven clips of ammo.

"I made a promise to your dad that I would protect you," he said. "This is the best I can do for now."

"I don't need protection. I have everything I need," Hilo said. "I feel safer here than anywhere. If all hell breaks loose, I can head underground and survive."

"You don't understand, Hilo. Your position and your safety have been compromised. Ms. Snicth and I have tried to keep you safe for as many years as possible, but a message was transmitted by someone inside that knows who you are. Someone with access to those damn computers. We can no longer promise your safety, and we have to move," said Mr. Freewheel. "I'll be back once I gather more supplies."

~

Hilo was arguing loudly, demanding Billionaire Robert Fencewood leave FSFS. She did not want to implement the chip reader that would replace cash. She ran into Robert Fencewood inside FSFS when she went to get things in order for her return after everything went back to normal. She did not know about the Crown Virus 2019 pandemic yet. She only knew that the chip used with the Chiptech software bore the mark of the Anti-Savior.

Before Robert Fencewood finally left FSFS, he removed a familiar object from inside of his brief-case. Hilo's eyes widened when he donned his yellow-striped fedora, and she finally realized she had just discovered that the Chiptech CEO, Robert Fencewood, was her mother's killer. Fencewood wore a knowing grin and pompously exited FSFS. Hilo stood in shock. Though speechless, she knew that she was gonna kill Robert Fencewood that night.

She went to her private lesson with Professor U. to clear her mind and prepare for hand-to-hand combat.

~

I waited at the Interlandmass Airport for my flight. It was beginning to get dark that calm, spring evening when a message played over the airport intercom. "Due to InterLandmass quarantine, no flights are scheduled out of any Landmass at this time.

Only essential businesses will remain open—grocery and gas convenient stores. Please return home and stay inside to stop the spread of the Interlandmass Crown Virus 2019." At the first mention of the word virus, my palms grew sweaty, and I was trying to take in fewer breaths of air. I went to gather my rifle from baggage claim and was denied because I lacked proper identification and was technically no longer considered a Newtop citizen. "Damn virus and damn I.D.'s!" I said to the representative at the baggage counter. "I thought that everyone had the right to bear arms. That's what us Newtop Landmass citizens are supposed to believe in! It's written into the damn Landmass Constitution!" I yelled as I walked away, deflated once more. On top of that, I had just learned that I was unable to travel because my identification card did not have the newly implemented facial recognition photo referred to as Realpic ID.

I stared outside the windows of the Interlandmass Airport and noticed something that was not easily recognizable. It was a giant eye made out of large, lamplit wooden poles and a small patch of sand. It was ugly, and one had to be at a high vantage point to see it, but knowing what I knew, the large eye literally stared me in the face. I recalled the symbols I had come across in one of Hilo's books. I already missed Hilo.

My thoughts of Hilo were interrupted when I heard a voice I had just become familiar with.

"Henry, I am pleased to have found you here. I understand that flights are cancelled at the moment. It is the perfect time to discuss the details of your book publishing deal. Please, follow me," said Mr. Bookman.

Mr. Bookman and I walked down the airport lobby towards the elevators. We took the elevator down to the lowest level where the airport subway system was. I watched the rail carts pass by. We walked to the far end of the subway where there was a ticket booth. We entered and to my surprise, Mr. Bookman pushed a button and the floor started descending. We were in a secret elevator going further under the Interlandmass Airport.

"What you have written is interesting, to say the least," Mr. Bookman said, then he grinned his wolfish grin.

"Thank you. I am happy that we are gonna move forward with the publishing deal. I could really use the money," I said.

The elevator hit the lowest level, which was far beneath the airport. We walked out of the ticket booth and started towards a room that looked like it was lit by candles. The flames were flickering—as candles do—but the flickers weren't normal. The thought had not crossed my mind that I was heading toward danger. The only thing on my mind was making money, and then going to apologize to Hilo.

As we approached the entrance to the room, I could hear chanting. My curiosity got the best of me, and we kept walking towards the sound.

"Your book is worth more than you know, Henry. That is why we have come to my personal office," Mr. Bookman said, as we stood in the entrance of the room. "Not many know about its existence below ground."

"Seems like an interesting place to operate your business," I said, scanning the strange landscape in front of me. It looked like a modern facility, lit by burning white candles of all sizes. Candle wax oozed slowly onto the floor. I wondered how long it had been under the Interlandmass Airport and who had built it.

"The Secret of Shadows is important to the Establishments of every Landmass," he said, as we entered the orange-glowing room. It was decorated in ancient symbols and lined with many statues, which I could only think were idols that the S.O.S. worshipped. There were many robed men chanting, shrouded in shadow. I thought they were floating. My eyes widened when Mr. Bookman turned to me and said, "So important that I would like you to sign your publishing deal with your blood."

A gentleman dressed in a red suit silently approached, extending a warm hand, and with a charming look he gestured for me to walk towards the center of the room. There was a stone table with pictographs engraved on the side. Hilo was standing next to a man in black wearing a yellow-striped fedora, Robert Fencewood, and another masked man. Hilo standing there gave me more courage, even though she was bound and gagged with rope. I knew I needed to save her. But my courage and my hopes of saving Hilo disappeared when Fencewood and the other masked man dragged Hilo down a back room. I wondered where it led to.

"This is Rey Apleon," said Mr. Bookman. "He will soon rule this world. He is the one who will gather your blood for your contract."

~

Mr. Freewheel and Ms. Snicth finished gathering supplies. Upon approaching FSFS, they saw flames coming out from behind the market. "Oh shit..." Mr. Freewheel whispered underneath his breath. "Hilo."

Chapter 9

I punched Rey in the face with a couple jabs and a right cross, putting my weight behind the punches with my legs, like Mr. Freewheel instructed. Mr. Bookman double-legged me and took me to the ground. I was excited and pumped, and we grappled for what seemed like forever. I had no clue that this bastard had been trained by the best military in the world. He countered all of my attacks efficiently and expertly. I remembered my training with Professor U. and told myself to relax. I jumped to Mr. Bookman's back, and Rey landed a crushing kick to my skull.

Dizzy, I couldn't hang onto my seatbelt grip and fell to the ground. Rey went for another kick, but I expected it. Freewheel taught us to always expect dirty blows, especially when an enemy is on the ground. I blocked the kick with both arms and drove in for a sloppy double leg. I took down the red-suited man and focused my attention on Mr. Bookman. He went for a single leg of his own, and I countered with hammer fists to the back of his head. Rey stood up quickly and ran to aid Mr. Bookman. The two lifted me up, one man for each of my legs, and slammed me hard onto the stone floor. I was winded, but my adrenaline was pumping and the thrill of the fight for my life gave me strength.

I thought I saw Justin and Anne-Marie watching as Mr. Bookman rolled to my back and dirtied his white suit from the dusty floor. He placed both hooks on my hips and secured a tight rear naked choke. Rey got up and unsheathed a dagger that looked ancient.

I heard explosions coming from all around. Hooded monks were splattered across the entire room. Remains colored the walls. More explosions came, and I heard whistles whizzing by and the rata-tat-tat of automatic machine guns.

"Get your ass up, Henry!" yelled Mr. Freewheel. To my surprise, I saw Ms. Snicth. We looked at each other for a brief moment, and she smiled. She looked beautiful with a smile, I thought. I couldn't help but smile back, even though I was in Mr. Bookman's death grip. I must have looked funny.

With a free hand, the one that wasn't wrapped tightly around my neck, Mr. Bookman grabbed a silver revolver and pointed it to my temple. Even though the room was lit by torches and candlelight, the power shut off completely under the Interlandmass Airport, then came on like a flash of lightning. From the corner of my left eye, I saw Rey run out the back door, and I thought I saw Justin smile from across the room. He disappeared, and I thought I was seeing things. Possibly an illusion caused from either the tight choke from behind or the blow to my head. It didn't matter. I knew I was going to black out and eventually die. All of this for not paying attention, I thought. I should've listened to Hilo and left the damn Tivoli Tavern. Money didn't matter to me at that moment.

I heard more explosions and felt warm blood trickling down my neck. Someone wailed, and I couldn't tell who it was. All I knew was that I was as good as dead. Blood was all over Mr. Bookman's white suit, and I knew it was mine. I thought I saw demons floating in the air in front of me.

～

There were IIXX markings all over the doors and hallways that led from under the Interlandmass Airport toward another sacrificial alter under the library at The College. Hilo knew she was under Computer City because there were many wires connected to a blue glowing power source. It smelled like a sterile room, and there were cameras hooked up to video tape her death. Hilo tried to wiggle free as Fencewood and the masked man dragged her into a room beneath Computer City.

"The cycle will be complete once we sacrifice you. I call it the trinity," Robert Fencewood said, while he and the masked man slammed Hilo hard onto the stainless steel table. The table had drain holes that led to a plastic container. She knew it was to collect her blood. These bastards drank it like vampires at their secret parties. She knew the giants ate humans, and anybody possessed by their demons would enjoy humans as well. She began to realize that the freezer along the wall was probably for her body parts. *Sick bastards*, she thought.

The masked man started laughing, unsettling Hilo.

I was running away from the sacrificial room underneath the Interlandmass Airport. Ms. Snicth and Mr. Freewheel ran beside me. We ran down a long, narrow hallway. I had no idea that all of this existed beneath the Island. There were many markings on the tunnel walls. I noticed most of them were from the Ventidos and many pictures depicted the Sinpaz. There were intricate paintings of the fallen Innumerable Lights and the Ventidos gathering on the Mount to discuss their plan against HUB. Pictures of mythological creatures walking amongst men. Giants holding large blocks of stone that were gathered next to an unfinished Stone Triangle Temple. Everything started to make sense. My clothes were stained in Mr. Bookman's blood, and I was confident that we were heading to save Hilo. I felt very brave, even though I was scared shitless.

We burst through a door engraved with the Ventidos numerals right before Hilo was almost stabbed through the heart by the masked man. "Prepare to die, Commander Henzo Yookimura!" Ms. Snicth screamed.

The masked man laughed a familiar laugh, which shook me to my core. I recognized his laugh and knew who it was even though he was wearing a mask. He ripped off the mask, and my heart sank. I had never been betrayed before, but I finally understood how The Savior felt when He was given up by one of His own friends to be captured and put to death. Professor U. laughed a crazy laugh, and he lost all of my respect. I was completely angered but tried to think things through in the moment. Hilo was still gagged and tied down to a grey table. Ms. Snicth and Mr. Freewheel started shooting. Robert Fencewood and Professor U. dodged the bullets at the speed of light. They moved faster than any creature known to man and were nearing the opening of the white room with guns of their own.

"To hell with you fucking bastards!" screamed Mr. Freewheel, as he began emptying a full clip from his assault rifle, spraying bullets in all directions.

I sprinted towards Hilo while Ms. Snicth and Mr. Freewheel fought off the possessed, remaining members of Advanced Special Operations Unit Team 1. I untied her as quickly as possible and, as she sat up, she ripped the gag off her mouth. Her face was lined in pink from where the rope cut off her circulation. I felt bad for her. At that moment she smiled at me, and I felt the courage to kiss her. We kissed for the first time, and I knew inside of me that everything was going to be okay. Hilo was safe, and Mr. Freewheel and Ms. Snicth could take care of Fencewood and Professor U.

We were running towards a ladder that led to a trap door. I knew it must have led to the teacher's lounge under Computer City. I let Hilo go first. It took everything in me to respect her and not look up her black skirt. Hilo got to the top and pushed up on the trap door, climbing into the lounge. At the top, she turned and reached down to grab my hand.

I turned and saw Justin and Anne-Marie enter the sterile, white room. Everything went dark.

Chapter 10

When I finally woke, I saw Anne-Marie looking over me. I heard her telling someone everything would be all right. I saw Hilo smile, though it looked as if she were staring at me through an invisible barrier. I knew I must have been in the hospital at The College. I saw Mr. Freewheel and Ms. Snicth dragging two men behind them, their eyes wide open and their mouths gaping—never to close again. I was so pissed at finding out that Professor U. was Henzo Yookimura. He'd betrayed both Hilo and me. Although he was dead, I felt mixed emotions. I was happy Hilo and I were safe and that the leaders of the Sellers of Souls were dead. On the other hand, I knew we had started a war with an enemy that had reached high up in the powers of the world. We hadn't captured their real leader, Rey Apleon.

Hilo smiled, and I knew she was looking at me. Anne-Marie started talking. I wondered where Justin was.

"The Great War has started, Henry. You're lucky Hilo saved a copy of your book. Her entire library was burned down, but she saved a copy to preserve the truth. She is going to share it with the world," Anne-Marie said. It was strange because I had never heard her talk so much before.

"Rey Apleon has taken his seat upon The Great Temple and proclaimed himself HUB. Almost everyone in the world believes he is 'the savior' because he put an end to the pandemic and feeds them with both food and false truths," Anne-Marie said. "Everyone wears the Anti-Savior's mark in their right hand or their foreheads. FSFS was destroyed."

"I'm dreaming," I said to Anne-Marie. I wasn't paying full attention to what she was saying.

"Yes, you are, and you must wake," Anne-Marie said to me.

"Where am I?" I asked her.

"The First World."

Chapter 11

I saw the beginning of time up to the end. It was like watching a movie on widescreen that flipped through scenes. We were riding spotted horses as I watched. There were colors and creatures all around me that were difficult to describe. I saw a pride of lions walking next to sheep. I saw a glowing light, but it wasn't from any sun—it was a million times brighter. There were other people laughing, along with winged creatures sitting next to a waterfall. I saw a tree with fruit on it that was guarded by a sword that pointed in all directions. As we approached the tree, an angel appeared and congratulated me. I was allowed to grab one fruit from the tree of life. I ate it. It tasted like nothing I have ever had. I knew I would never have to eat again. All of my wants disappeared, and I felt alive for the first time.

I watched on the widescreen in the sky when HUB and the Word spoke. When the first light appeared. I knew that was the same light that permeated throughout the First World. I saw the celebration of the angels at the first announcement of The Savior's name. I saw Him from when He was born to when He was killed by men for being sinless and proclaiming the truth. "I forgive you," I heard The Savior say on another screen as He died. I saw Him rise again to the First World three days later. I saw His Holy Spirit extend out to everyone who called upon His name thereafter. I finally understood that HUB did not understand His greatest creation—mankind—until He experienced walking amongst them. It was about empathy. It was about love. I saw and finally understood everything.

I saw the 200 Innumerable Lights, known as the Sinpaz, fall from the sky and their 22 leaders corrupt the world. I saw Enek talking to the Ventidos, telling them a message sent from HUB: "You have no peace." I finally understood the meaning of Sin Paz. Without Peace. I saw the Great Drowning and the giants that were killed from it. I saw creatures that were of mixed DNA, created by the S.O.S. under the instruction of the Sinpaz. I watched giants build the Stone Triangle Temples across the Seven Landmasses. I saw the 1st King, Rey Apleon, try to build a tower to destroy HUB. I saw the tower get destroyed, and the New People confounded by many languages. I saw them scattered to every corner of the Seven Landmasses. I saw the 1st King's mummification. I saw the freezing of the Frozen Waters at the end of the world, the Arctic Ring. I saw HUB trap the Ventidos—the 22 leaders of the Sinpaz—in the frozen waters. I saw demons flee the dead giants' bodies, which floated in the Great Drowning flood waters. I saw the women the Sinpaz mated with turn into sirens. I saw the S.O.S. emerge years later and discover ancient texts. I saw the creation of the World Church and the Holy Campaign, where all texts were discovered and hidden underground. I saw the altering of the Old Book. I saw the book burnings and the reason for the Census Killings. I knew it was a sacrifice to the Ventidos. I saw Rey Apleon leading the New Landmass Order and the World Church, governing every Landmass under a One World Agreement. The world was united under one religion and one currency. I saw people being chipped with his mark and other people being sentenced to death for not accepting it. I saw the great tribulation. I saw a burning lake of fire on one of the screens down the way. Wailing souls from the unforgiven filled another screen. I saw the Ventidos cast into the Lake of Fire along with Rey Apleon and the rest of the demons and the Sinpaz. I was trying to see more of what happened at the end of the world when Anne-Marie spoke.

"Shortly after the day you passed on from the New World, there was worldwide destruction from dissension, separation, and propaganda. It was connected to the pandemic, which originated at Billionaire Robert Fencewood's Nutrisource. Now you know that everything was designed to implement the mark of the Anti-savior—the chip. Fencewood's Nutrisource seed bank was acquired by the New Landmass Order and is still virtually inaccessible. Anyone unwilling to accept the chip—unable to grow their own food because there are no seeds left in the Seven Landmasses—eventually starved to death," Anne-Marie said. "Cash was replaced by the chip designed at Chiptech because most people feared the spread of germs. It was labeled dangerous and nonessential because many feared that it could carry and spread another 2019 Crown Virus. The chip was placed in the right hand or forehead, as prophesied in the Old Book."

"What happened to FSFS?" I asked.

"FSFS eventually shut down because Hilo refused to implement the chip scanners needed to buy, sell, and trade," Anne-Marie explained. "Only businesses that had the chip technology were allowed to operate."

We were riding spotted horses as she talked. I was silent and didn't feel like I was dead. I just felt like time ceased to exist. I felt like a blindfold had been removed from my eyes. There was a rainbow in the heavens. *This is forever*, I thought. I wondered where Justin was. Most of all, I wondered how Hilo was doing and what time it was back in the New World. Part of me wasn't worried about her because I knew she understood how to survive. She carried with her sacred knowledge and was very resourceful. Ultimately, I knew that she could take care of herself.

As we approached an area where nimbus rain-clouds surrounded a massive cliff edge, I saw an army of one hundred times one hundred thousand archangels seated upon warhorses. I saw their leader, The Savior, sitting on a radiant warhorse, larger than any warhorse across the universe. It was impressive. The Savior had His name written on a patch that was on His right leg. It read: The Word. I looked up from His name patch and recognized

The Savior. I recognized His dark features, His eyes like blazing fire. It was Justin. He was looking over what looked like a snow globe. I knew He was looking into the New World. I approached with Anne-Marie to see what He was looking at.

I saw Hilo reading a tattered paperback book to a small band of rebels. She was strong and beautiful. The events that occurred in the New World had toughened her like iron sharpens iron. I saw Ms. Snicth and Mr. Freewheel standing guard with fully loaded weapons by Hilo's side. When Hilo finished speaking, I saw the small rebel army raise their arms, holding their weapons high, as they let out a battle cry. Apparently, what she had just read inspired them. I noticed the book she referenced was mine. For a long moment, she was staring at a picture of me that she'd taped inside the book. A tear fell from her eye as she slid the book into her war vest. By the looks of her, Hilo knew that she was going to lose. But she also knew that it was better to die having lived each and every day standing up for the truth—staying strong to her beliefs. Most of all, Hilo knew love, the greatest commandment. She had my name written in her heart. I saw that she carried it inside of her each day after my death.

Against all odds, Hilo's army stood unwavering against the entire world. I saw an evil army, one million times bigger than the small band of rebels, completely surrounding the small band of rebels from all sides. I saw the leader of the enemy army, the great deceiver. It was the red-suited man, Rey Apleon. The entire world—the ones that were chipped—turned to salute the great deceiver. The evil army was completely silent when they turned back to face Hilo's army. They let out no battle cry. I saw evil spirits circling above and slithering in and out of the men who were part of the enemy army. I wanted to rid my mind of their unsightly features. The entire sight—the enemy army, the Sinpaz, the demons—was ominous. Shadowed in emptiness. Dark as the bottomless pit.

I was glad when I noticed Mr. and Mrs. Eden watching proudly as their daughter was assembling the small rebel army for the Great Battle in the New World. I could see tears of joy falling from their eyes. Mr. Eden held Mrs. Eden close. I locked that sight in my mind.

The Savior stepped off from His magnificent warhorse. He reached for something that was hung from His warhorse and walked over to me.

I dismounted my spotted horse and approached Him. We hugged. He smiled at me like a proud father.

"What's this?" I asked, as He handed me the wrapped-up bundle.

"Your armor," He said. With a bow of respect and appreciation, I took the bundle. "We're going to help Hilo," The Savior said to me, still wearing the proud smile.

I opened the bundle of armor. I put it on expertly like a warrior spreading war paint along his face. On my right leg was my name patch. It said: Henry Gomez, Prophet. The Savior handed me my sword. I pulled it from its sheath. There was a glowing word imprinted along the blade that said, "Truth."

I couldn't stop staring at the shimmering blade. The Savior mounted His warhorse. He turned to face the great army of archangels. After sheathing my sword and mounting my spotted warhorse, I fell in line next to Anne-Marie. I felt like I should've known all along that Anne-Marie was an angel. I also felt silly for thinking she was anyone's girlfriend. At that moment, I finally understood that Anne-Marie was *my* guardian angel. She was beautiful. She had always been. She simply smiled at me, and we turned to hear The Savior speak.

The Savior raised His sword, and with a voice that spread across the heavens, He spoke and the sky broke open. It sounded like the first Word that created life. It sounded like a million mountains crashing into a million waves. Like thunder clapping, applauding the death of a billion stars exploding at once. His voice shook every pillar across every realm. I saw every creature quiver. In His great voice, like the sound of rushing waters, The Savior said, "It's Time."

Afterword

Henry knew he had done his best. Though his book was considered illegal, it was secretly uploaded onto the Shadow Pages of The Network. And even with extreme censorship—with most books and information destroyed throughout the world—his legend grew, along with news that there was a physical copy of a book that helped expose the truth floating around. In every Landmass, at least a few copies existed and were spread amongst rebels standing up against the New Landmass Order to further the righteous cause.

Henry smiled upon his spotted horse. He gave his life so that Hilo could live and spread the truth. No gift was greater than a person giving up their life for another. She was a better rebel leader than a grocery store owner, Henry thought. His smile lingered while he sat upon his spotted horse when he realized he had helped initiate the Great Battle, and his short book helped build the small rebel army. He had achieved greatness despite impossible odds. Henry realized that the entire purpose of his life was complete. He had written The Savior's name in the dedication of his unpublished, first book. It was dedicated to all of us. It was titled, *Know Seeds*. Henry rode down with The Savior from above the clouds to conquer and destroy the enemy, his sword of truth held high. At the end of the Great Battle, every knee bowed to The Savior.

www.ingramcontent.com/pod-product-compliance
Lightning Source LLC
Chambersburg PA
CBHW030749110726
47900CB00008B/2521